BEHIND the Wildflowers

T.J. DEAL

Copyright © 2025 by TJ Deal

All rights reserved

No part of this book may be reproduced, distributed, or transmitted in any form or by any means, including photocopying, recording, or other electronic or mechanical methods, without the prior written permission of the author, except in the case of brief quotations in a book review.

This is a work of fiction. Names, characters, places, and incidents are the product of the author's imagination or are used fictitiously. Any resemblance to actual events, locales, or persons, living or dead, is coincidental.

ISBN: 979-8-9907007-8-9

Cover design by: Sarah Hansen © Okay Creations

Editor: Sam Moon

Developmental editor: Matthew Deal

To the audacious and badass women who aren't afraid to bite off more than they can chew, and figure out how to fucking chew it as they go.

Prologue

Cruising toward Bend, the sunset paints the mountains gold—kind of how I feel inside: nervous, excited, scared, but mostly thrilled. Summer's long days make the late drive feel natural, almost timeless.

The only thing on my mind is Sienna—my newly established girlfriend that I can't seem to get enough of—her laugh, her intelligence. She's got this dark red hair that reminds me of the natural garnet necklace my mom used to wear—deep, rich, and shining with understated elegance. It was the first thing I noticed about her, like my mom was sending me a message saying, *This is it. She could be the one.* She's shorter than me, but about average in height, and those hazel-green eyes—God, her eyes—so full of life. Needless to say, I'm falling for her, falling hard and fast.

Last-minute, she invited me over tonight, and I jumped at the chance to spend time with her. I live for these rare moments —those few hours a week we get together—that make all the busy days worth it. We're both students at the community college in Bend—me studying paramedicine, her for dental assisting—and we are both working full-time.

We've only been dating a few months, and she just dropped a bomb on me: she's pregnant. I still can't wrap my head around the thought of me being a dad, but here we are.

The road blurs, and suddenly, I'm transported back to a few weeks ago.

We're sitting in my truck, just the two of us, parked in the trees on the edge of campus. It's the beginning of summer, birds chirping, and the warm sunlight filtering through the leaves. It should've been our little break from everything else, but from the moment she got in, I could tell something was off. She doesn't beat around the bush, though. First thing she says is, "I'm pregnant."

Everything in me stills for a second as I scan her face, trying to figure out if she's joking or serious. Fear hits me first—like a punch out of nowhere, with the hows, whys, and holy shits racing through my head. But once I snap out of it, I see her shoulders softly shaking. Then I notice tears starting to stream down her face. Without thinking, I pull her close, rub her back, trying to make sense of everything.

"Hey, hey," I whisper, my voice steady despite all the chaos going on inside. "It's okay. We'll figure this out."

Only my words bounce back at me, like they aren't even registering with her. She starts crying harder, clutching her stomach, devastation pouring out of her as if this is the worst news possible. I don't get her reaction, though. Yeah, it's not what I was expecting, but that doesn't mean it's bad news.

"Are you... are you mad at me?" she asks, her voice breaking through tears.

"No, Sienna. Never. I—" My voice catches. "Why would I be mad at you?"

She looks at me, eyes red and desperate. "I didn't mean for this to happen, Levi, I swear. I've been on birth control... I don't even know how far along I might be—"

"Hey, it's okay," I cut her off softly. "We'll figure out all the details. A doctor will know for sure."

She nods, still trembling. "I just... I haven't been with anyone for over a year, Levi. I swear. It's yours."

Realization dawns on me. She thought I'd have an entirely different reaction— accuse her, blame the situation on her, whatever else douchebags do in situations like this.

I squeeze her hand. "The baby not being mine wasn't even a thought. We're in this together. You, me, the baby."

We try to do some math, guessing how far along she could be, but she keeps shaking her head. Turns out she's been taking birth control the whole time, which makes things even more confusing.

She sniffles, then looks at me anxiously. "Will the baby be okay? Like, is birth control somehow poisoning it?"

God, I want to tell her she doesn't have to worry about that. My knowledge might be limited as a paramedic-to-be, but I know this: I want this little one.

"I don't know," I say softly.

"What if I've been hurting him or her?" she asks, voice trembling again.

I want to reassure her, but all I can do is shrug. "We'll make an appointment, first thing, and they'll make sure the baby is healthy. Okay? One step at a time."

She looks over, biting her lip. "Do you think your family will hate me?"

"No! Dan's going to be mad I beat him to the punch, but he'll be happy if I'm happy." That's the thing about twins—we may fight over anything we can, but when it comes down to it, there isn't anyone I trust more than him. Womb mates, roommates, and now the best mates. Or whatever the saying is.

She nods. "And your dad? What about my mom? They're both going to freak out."

That thought stops the memory cold, and I have to shake it off and refocus on the road. I don't know how my dad will feel about me becoming a dad so young and out of wedlock. I do know my dad's a good man—the sheriff of this little town, the kind of guy everyone trusts. He'll want me to step up and be there, no matter what. But I'm pretty sure my recent mess hasn't been sitting well with him.

Last month, I lost it. Caught some lowlife trying to sexually assault a friend of mine. I didn't just get angry—I saw red. Almost killed the guy, but Sienna stopped me. My knuckles still sting from the punches thrown, but I'd do it again in a heartbeat.

And the trouble with her mom? Yeah, that's a whole other story. She's a nurse at the hospital, was working on the guy I beat up—and refused to talk to me afterward. Said I wasn't good enough for Sienna. Maybe I'm not.

I'm still a student, working crazy hours as an EMT, although I'm almost done. Once I pass my exam, I'll be able to get licensed. With any luck, that'll be a couple of months before the baby is born.

I run a hand through my hair, trying to breathe.

"Stop," I command into the silence. "Sienna is safe and

healthy. That's all that matters. Everything else will work itself out."

After a few moments, Sienna's voice echoes in my head—soft and determined— and I'm back that day, listening to her gush about our baby.

———

"I already love this little one," she admits. "My mom will get over it. I know you have a good heart. It'll just take time."

I zone in on her words. "You already love it?"

She nods, looks at me with that little sparkle in her eyes, and says, "Is that crazy? I just keep imagining a little boy that looks just like you."

I can't help but preen a little at the thought, feeling a smile tug on my lips. Honestly, imagining that feels... right. As if it's meant to be. But then something else sneaks in, and I can't stop myself from saying it: "Or a little girl who looks just like you."

Her smile widens, and she leans her head on my shoulder. I can see she's already picturing it—the tiny baby with dark red hair and her hazel eyes.

"Wait," she says, her voice a little playful. "What about names? There are so many to pick from!"

"Well... uhm, if it's a boy, he has to be named Cal."

Her eyebrows shoot up. "Why?"

"I may have made a promise in high school—I'd name my firstborn son after Mr. Calvin. I called him Cal. He gave me enough extra credit to bump my grade from a high B to a low A... and I promised him I'd name my first kid after him if he did it."

"You're joking!" She looks at me like I'm crazy, but when she sees I'm not, she smiles anyway.

I tap my fingers on her shoulders, rhythmically. "No, Sienna, this isn't a joking matter." I try to say as seriously as I can. "It was *very* important to me to get straight A's throughout high school."

"Seriously?" she asks, cracking up.

"Yeah," I say, shrugging. "I was always kind of competitive about grades. Dan was the goodie-two-shoes—the one who never got into trouble. I was known as 'the troublemaker,' but I still made sure my GPA was better than his. Plus, that meant my dad couldn't complain much because I was always bringing home good grades."

She chuckles softly and leans against me. "That's actually... surprisingly endearing."

"Baby Cal—you okay with that?"

She pauses thoughtfully, then glances at me, a little teasing. "Sure, but what about a girl? Did you sign your soul away for that name, too?"

I burst out laughing. "No—I'm open to anything. Whatever feels right."

Her eyes soften again, and she nods. "Me too."

A beat of silence, then she looks at me, like she's gathering her courage. "Levi, I know this all happens so suddenly, and it's a lot to take in... but if I have to go through it with anyone, I'm really glad it's you."

Her words hit me right in the chest that day. There are a lot of women in the world I could never imagine raising a child with, but Sienna isn't one of them. She's light, warm, full of energy and smiles— but above all else, she's kind.

I pull into a parking space outside her apartment, excited to see her. The doctor appointment we went to last week said she was measuring around twenty-one weeks, which means she got pregnant pretty much the first time we had sex. Not ideal by any circumstances, but it makes sense. She's barely showing, which is actually the reason she took a test to begin with. At first, she thought she was bloated from the new birth control pills, and they were causing the weird symptoms she was having. But no—somehow, the timeline didn't work out. From when she thought she'd be protected to us having sex, it didn't add up. Add to that she was skipping the "sugar pills," experiencing occasional breakthrough bleeding—or what she thought was breakthrough bleeding—and here we are.

We opted to wait on finding out the gender; she wants to be surprised. But I'd be lying if I said I wasn't looking at that ultrasound wishing I knew how to read it.

Either way, she has the cutest little bump that I find my hand gravitating toward anytime we are together.

I make my way to the first-floor apartment she lives in, paid for by her dad, who's a surgeon in California. It seems as if they don't have much of a relationship, but beyond the basics, she avoids talking about him. It's a nice little one-bedroom, but I'm hoping I can convince her to move to Three Sisters with me. I already called a family friend— Lovey, who owns most of the rentals in Central Oregon— and asked if she had anything available. She's setting me up with a modest two-bedroom house on the outskirts of town.

My knuckles rap on the door, a smile spreading on my face. I genuinely like Sienna, and although this is a confusing time, spending time with her is the best. She's funny and light-hearted, making jokes that are funnier than most of my friends. Even Dan likes her— thinks she's a good fit to match my energy. Which says a lot, considering I don't think he's ever liked a girl I've brought home.

After a minute of her not answering, I knock again and step

back. She texted me less than thirty minutes ago and said she was excited to see me, so I know she's here. I tune my ears to listen inside, but there's nothing on the other side of the door. When she still doesn't come out, I pull out my phone and hit the call button.

Dread hits me instantly when I hear it ringing on the other side. My fist pounds on the door, worry hitting me like a freight train.

She still doesn't come.

I try for the handle, and with ease it opens, but what I never expected to see is Sienna on the floor, lying on her side.

I run to her, dropping to my knees immediately. My training takes over. I check her responsiveness—no reaction. Her eyes are dilated, skin warm and clammy. She's unresponsive, no pulse. My heart races— I dial 911 and start CPR, pushing hard, fast.

"911..."

"Medical emergency, pregnant woman found unconscious at the Stone Butte Apartment Complex, #104."

Dispatch relays instructions, telling me to stay calm, but I'm in the zone. My focus shifts from her chest to her open mouth.

Come on, Levi. Stay focused. Save her.

I lose track of time—maybe a minute, maybe five. The crew arrives behind me, and I keep pumping.

"Turner?" I don't have to look to recognize Josiah's voice. I've trained as much as I could over the last few years with Deschutes County Fire and Rescue, as well as worked in my own neighboring county, Cascadia.

I repeat what I told dispatch, never losing rhythm, even though sweat drips from my brow. "Unresponsive when I arrived, found her here, 22 weeks pregnant..."

His hand grips my shoulder, relieving me from my duty so they can take over, but I don't want to stop.

"We've got it, son. You can ride—let's go."

I fall back on my haunches and let them work. Within a minute, they have her loaded, and I'm in the captain's seat as they continue treatment. Josiah is operating the LUCAS chest compression device, and I can only watch from what feels like a distance beyond my body's reach— as if I've hoisted myself above the chaos, observing the scene with a detached clarity that's almost surreal.

Her heart is beating on its own by the time we arrive at the hospital, but she's still not awake. Barely breathing, but she made it—that's all I can focus on.

They take her behind the doors, and I'm left standing in the waiting room, feeling numb. My body remains still, in shock from what just happened, but somehow I manage to sit.

Right when I'm about to ask for an update, a wild mane of red hair pulled into a sleek bun bursts out of the ICU doors. I recognize her immediately—Sienna's mom.

Anger and pain radiate from her body, and when she sets her sights on me, I know it's all going to be directed at me.

"Get the fuck out! You don't belong here!" she screams.

I stand up, my hands rising in a plea. "I didn't—"

"You did! That baby caused a P.E., and it's your fault she's pregnant!"

"P.E.?" It hits me—pulmonary embolism. It can cause sudden cardiac arrest and stop her heart, or severe hypoxia, depriving the brain of oxygen. She'd have been gone by the time I got there. Nothing I could've done would have saved her. But— her heart was beating again in the ambulance. I saw it with my own two eyes.

"She's gone! Because of you, she's as good as dead!" Her

fists hit my chest, and I don't even care that it hurts. I'm still reeling from her words.

"As good as dead? But—the baby," I say, disbelief thick in my voice, as a security guard approaches, wrapping his arms around her and pulling her back.

"You killed them." Her last words echo in my mind. I fall to my knees, my body shuddering with disbelief. *Did I really do this? Is this my fault?*

Chapter One

Aubrey

OH. MY. GOD.

"Cal Sullivan Dubrow!" I nearly come unglued as I step out of my room into what can only be described as an art war zone. I'd been in my makeshift work studio—no more than an hour or two—and now, in the dining room, my normally tidy twelve-year-old nephew has turned chaos into an art form. Art supplies are spilled everywhere—across the table, the floor, even draped over the chairs. Paper scraps flutter like confetti, and I can already feel a headache brewing as I imagine cleaning up this mess.

Thank God my mom's in Florida. If there's one thing about Rosa Dubrow, it's that she cannot handle chaos—and this? This is chaos.

"Aunnie! I've got to finish this project by tomorrow!"

"Okay—but what's with all the glitter?" I reach out, catching a shimmer of blue floating down. "Is that... feathers?"

Glaring at the poster board in front of him, he fumed, "It's supposed to be colorful."

"Oh, it's definitely colorful," I reply, leaning in to get a better look. He's been working on this project for weeks—the writing portion—but I can tell the decorating part has been saved for the last minute.

"It looks good, Cal," I say softly, trying to reassure him.

The poster's about family history—our heritage. A big photo of him sits in the center, but aside from that, there are no labels or photos of the other family members. My heart sinks as I realize why: Cal doesn't want to explain the complicated story of his mom's death and his dad's abandonment.

A flicker of rage sparks inside me—Cal deserves so much more. But I swallow it down, focusing instead on the good.

On the left side, he's dedicated space to my dad—his grandfather—whom he's never met—and to our Ashkenazi Jewish roots. "The Dubrows" is scrawled boldly, with Germany and the U.S. listed underneath. Two weeks ago, I sat with Cal and helped him piece together what little I remember from my dad's stories about our ancestors: family leaving Germany before the war, immigrating to America, surviving struggles and triumphs as Jewish immigrants. I wish I could talk to my grandmother now—to understand those stories for real—but she passed away when I was close to Cal's age.

The right side honors my mom's side: Irish from County Cork and Native American from the Choctaw Nation. It's a mix that reflects us—a colorful tapestry of history and ethnicity.

Basically, his mother and I were born a unique blend of Jewish, Irish, and Native American heritage, and we both inherited different parts of each. I look more like my dad, with olive skin and dark brown eyes, while Sienna resembled our mother's "Sullivan" side more—fair skin, green eyes, and a dappling of freckles. If it weren't for our high cheekbones and gemstone-red hair, we might not have even looked related.

And yet, Cal didn't get any of that—he's the spitting image of his dad. I only met Levi once, when Sienna was dating him, but he didn't look like anything special—blonde, blue eyes, tall. The stereotypical Southern California surfer boy that our mom moved us away from a few years prior.

Cal doesn't know any of that though. He doesn't even know who his dad is—a promise I made my mother years ago. He's asked a few times, but I've always dodged it.

If Levi didn't want to be involved, then screw him. My dad pulled the same disappearing act, and I'm not about to let Cal experience that kind of rejection. He's better off never knowing a father who doesn't care than having one who pretends to care only to vanish when things get tough.

"Aunnie..." Cal's eyes meet mine nervously. "Do you think anyone will notice I left out my dad's side?"

My body tenses for a heartbeat as I scramble for the right words. "I... I don't know. Do you have the handout? Do you know if it's supposed to say exactly where your heritage comes from?"

He digs into a binder tossed on a nearby chair, then produces a piece of paper and hands it to me.

I glance over it and immediately feel relief—it doesn't specify which side of the family the heritage needs to be from.

"You should be fine," I say, giving him what I hope is a reassuring smile as I hand the paper back. "If anyone asks, just say you put the cool side of the family down."

He rolls his eyes but I catch a flicker of relief on his face.

"Grandma will think it's awesome, too. We can send her a picture of you with it after you present tomorrow." My mom signed a contract to become a travel nurse nearly two years ago, entrusting Cal to me because the pay was too good to miss. She visits between transfers, and we've even gone to visit her in each place she's been, but I know she's missing him.

He looks at me with a deadpan expression, and I can't help but laugh.

"I mean, maybe not the Dubrow side, but she'll LOVE the Sullivan side."

"She's gonna hate it," he laughs, then starts to mimic in a higher, mocking voice—like my mom—"Bubbe Dubrow was too highfalutin for a woman whose son didn't even know his—"

"Okay! Okay!" I interrupt him, not wanting him to finish that sentence. Unfortunately, my mother's never been very candid about her feelings toward my dad.

His grin widens, then suddenly falls. Without a word, he quickly turns back to his project and starts fidgeting with one of the decals.

"What?" I ask, nudging him gently.

He doesn't answer right away, but I can tell there is something bothering him.

"Cal, what?"

"Grandma called last night while you were in the shower," he finally says, voice hesitant.

"Okay?" I prod, wondering what could have caused that look on his face.

"She said not to tell you yet," he looks up, and I see worry flicker in his bright blue eyes. "You know how this is the last part of her contract?"

I nod, encouraging him to keep going. My mom signed a two-year contract and has been on a standard thirteen-week rotation. This post is her last before she comes home in seven weeks.

He swallows hard. "She said she got a job in Florida... and that we're moving there."

"She told you that?" My mind starts racing—first because, why is she talking to Cal about this and not me? And second... what the hell? Florida? Cal and I barely even liked Florida when we visited a few weeks ago.

He nods. "She's buying a house for us to live in—me and her."

My eyebrows shoot up. It finally begins to dawn on me—why she told Cal and not me. *She's cutting me out of the decision, not giving me a choice in the matter.* A swirl of fear and betrayal gnaws at me as I try to process everything.

"It has a pool," he adds quickly, "and she said the high school there is one of the best for football—and there are training camps for kids. So they're pretty much guaranteed to play college."

I nod, but inside, my mind's spinning, and my stomach's twisting in knots. This is happening so fast—too fast.

"But, Aunnie, I don't want to go... Can I—can I stay with you?" His voice cracks just a little at the end, his gaze pleading and vulnerable.

My mouth opens and closes, but words desert me as I scramble to find something—anything—that could comfort him. But no words come. Instead, my protective instincts flare fiercely—*what about Cal's feelings? What about mine?* She wants to rip us apart after spending every single day together for the last twelve years. The thought sparks a twinge of anger and helplessness that I can't seem to quiet.

"I'll talk to her," I say quickly, feeling a flicker of uncertainty as his eyes widen. I take a breath and calmly add, "Don't worry. I'll wait for her to tell me herself, or figure out what's really going on somehow."

He nods, then scowls at his giant poster board. Mumbling, "This is stupid."

I don't know if he's talking about the poster or the situation, but something in his tone tells me he doesn't want to elaborate.

Instead, I squeeze his shoulder gently. "Better not be talking about this cool-ass poster," I say with a faint smile.

"Come on, let's order enough Chinese food for an army—and while we wait for it to arrive, we can clean up this disaster."

He hesitates, then softly asks, "Movie night, too?"

"Heck-yes," I reply, trying to sound upbeat. "But nothing too long! It's a school night."

Cal ends up falling asleep halfway through the movie. I don't have the heart to wake him or move him, so I pause it and sit in the quiet instead.

What the hell is my mom thinking? And why isn't she talking to me about it?

Rather than losing my mind completely, I send a text to one of the few people I trust—Molly. Since my podcast gained popularity, I hired her to help me fact-check investigations. She began as my assistant, then became my executive producer, and now manages all those responsibilities and more. But she's also my best friend and the person I turn to when life gets crazy.

Molly Wick👑

> MOLLS! You'll never believe what Cal told me.

What?!

> My mom is trying to move him to FLORIDA.

> Without me!

> What the hell do I even do?

YOU'RE JOKING. She didn't even tell you?! CAL DID?! WTF? 😣 😖

But aren't you like legal guardian while she's been gone?

A heavy silence settles over me, feeling the weight of Cal's confession still hanging in the air. Maybe Molly is right—consulting a family attorney might be helpful—but do I really want to drag Cal through family court and risk destroying my relationship with my mom? *I don't know.*

Almost reflexively, I turn my phone back on, hoping a distraction will help—anything to quiet the jumble of thoughts swirling in my mind. My fingers scroll through emails—mostly ads, nothing interesting—until one message suddenly catches my attention.

From: LLincoln@EFSC.com

Subject: Inquiry Regarding Potential Irregularities—Mitchell and Walton Law Firm

Dear Aubrey Dubrow,

I am reaching out on behalf of the EFSC company, regarding an ongoing investigation into Mitchell and Walton Law Firm, based in Three Sisters, Oregon. Our team is conducting a comprehensive review of all cases associated with the firm to identify any possible criminal activity or irregularities.

During our inquiry, we've encountered birth records pertaining to an individual named Cal Dubrow that may have been altered. We've been trying to contact the mother, Rosa Dubrow, but have yet to receive a response. We are reaching out to next of kin and any other possible associates.

We kindly ask that if you have any relevant information or insights related to this matter, you contact me directly at your earliest convenience. Your cooperation is greatly appreciated and will assist in our investigation.

Thank you for your time and attention.

Sincerely,

L. Lincoln

Elite Forces Security and Contracting

My pulse pounds as I stare at the screen, a mix of shock and dread hitting me.

What in the hell is going on?

I read the email again, this time slowly, as if I need to understand each word individually.

Elite Forces Security and Contracting—Inquiry Regarding Potential Irregularities—Mitchell and Walton Law Firm.

The words blur for a moment as I process the gravity of the message: an investigation into alterations of Cal's birth records, apparently connected to Mitchell and Walton Law Firm. My mother is named as someone involved in 'potentially any possible criminal activity or irregularities.'

What did my mother do now?

Chapter Two

Levi

Sitting among the parents at my niece Ellie and nephew Ben's Jiu Jitsu class, I try not to let my age—the thirty-something, still single—gnaw at me. My eyes flick to the kids—tiny bodies twisting and tumbling on the mats. For a split second, my mind drifts to the woman I lost—and the baby I lost too. *Would he have been shy like Ben, or a fiery spark like Ellie?* No, no, no—I mentally put the lid back on the box. Twelve years of pretending it didn't hurt, of not going there—I've learned to shut that shit down fast. It's easier that way.

Instead, I refocus on what I do have—the absolute best niece and nephew. They're the spitting image of me—well, their dad too, but considering he's my identical twin, I get to claim their good looks. Our dad's genetics are freakishly strong; there's not an ounce of our mother's DNA in us—or of Olivia, in Ben and Ellie.

I watch on as Ben gets out of a hold by trapping this kids elbow and rolling him. If the coach hadn't broken down every move beforehand, I wouldn't believe Ben could do it so easily.

But in a blink, he's rolled the kid, who'd been holding him down, and is now on top.

Damn, Dan would've loved this—watching quiet Ben come out of his shell and stand up to a kid twice his size. *He should be the one here, cheering on his kids and supporting them, not me.*

A flicker of anger rolls through me, and I feel my shoulders tense, coiled like springs. *He should've known better—should've paid more attention. Got himself killed for what? Being too trusting, too kind, that's what.*

By the time I realize my jaw is clenched tight enough to chip a tooth, I'm watching the kids bow to their coach. *Shit, put the lid on box, Levi.*

Ben claps quietly and makes his way over to the Minecraft Crocs I bought him for his ninth birthday. Ellie, meanwhile, does a cartwheel on the mat, heading toward her sparkly shoes on the other side.

"Ellie, you gotta walk! We talked about this," Coach Johnson says, voice steady but tired.

She turns, flashing her sweetest grin. "Sorry, Coachie! Just so excited after the best class!"

He sighs heavily, but I catch a flicker of a grin trying to break through. Ellie dances her way over to us, full of energy, eyes shining.

"Ellie-smellie, you have to walk all the time in here," I say softly.

"Uncle Vi, it's not the pool! I won't slip or anything." A pang hits me—that she doesn't say 'or nothin'' anymore. I decide right then not to scold her more; someday she'll be too worried about what others think, and dancing or cartwheeling will fade away.

I glance at Ben, who just shrugs as if to say, 'What can we do? She's six.'

"Come on, you little rascals, let's get you home for T.N.T.D."

Ellie begins singing the lyrics we came up with a few years ago, her voice bright and full of energy:

"Because it's T.N.T.—Thursday Night Turner-Dinner,

T.N.T.—and I'll eat the food.

T.N.T.—I'm a power eater,

T.N.T.—watch me implode!"

I chuckle, the sound uplifting and familiar, but then I realize—now that we've added Olivia's new boyfriend, Drew, to the mix—it's probably time for a new name and song. Something Ellie and I love to do together. Usually, she and I belt it out loud, spinning lyrics and laughing, while Ben might toss out a line or two. But Ellie... Ellie's voice, always lively, always fearless, makes the song come alive with her own sparkle.

When we get to their house, I knock three times loudly, not out of politeness, but more to let them know we have arrived and they better get dressed—fast. A lesson I'm afraid we've learned the hard way. Thankfully, the kids are naive and had no idea why Olivia looked so frazzled with one boot on and the other thrown across the room. I, however, have never let them live it down.

"We're coming in!" I announce loudly as I open the door and step inside the large home that Olivia built from the ground up. After Dan died, she poured herself into this house, and it shows in every detail—careful touches, handmade decorations, and a warmth that fills every room. The kids may not understand the significance of her hard work, but I do, and I will always be grateful for her strength and resilience.

Olivia, with her brunette hair in a messy bun, wobbles around the corner. An apron covers her baby bump and red sundress. Her brown eyes crinkle with amusement as she tries to wipe her hands on a dish towel—her expression playful, like she has a secret.

"Sooo, you cooked?" I ask, eyeing her splattered apron and the chaos in the kitchen.

"I'm pregnant, not inept," she retorts with a smirk. "And you're eating it, so hush." Olivia is nearly eight months pregnant—an unexpected surprise that we're all excited about.

Behind her, Drew tries to hide a small smile. Taller than me, built like a lumberjack, he's in joggers and a T-shirt—more relaxed than I expected from a former Navy SEAL. There's a calm steadiness about him that I've come to appreciate, especially in how he treats Olivia and the kids with care and patience.

"What's on the menu tonight?" I ask, feigning curiosity while trying to ignore the odd smell still lingering in the air.

"Bacon-wrapped jalapeños, stuffed with peanut butter and topped with a drizzle of honey. Trust me, you'll love it," she says confidently, almost daring me. I exchange a hesitant glance with Drew, who shrugs.

"And the red sauce on your apron?" I prod, trying to keep it light.

Olivia looks down, then back at me, a broad grin spreading across her face. "Oh, that's just from the strawberry spaghetti I made earlier. It's an experimental dish, but I think it has potential."

"Strawberry spaghetti?" I mouth to Drew, who nods before shivering a little.

"Potential," he mouths back, giving me a faint, amused smile.

I can't shake the guilt stirring inside me for finding joy in Olivia's happiness with Drew. It's strange—wishing Dan was here to see her smile, yet feeling bound by loyalty to him and the marriage they shared. He wasn't the best husband—never gave her the attention she deserved—but he loved her with everything he had. I know he'd have wanted *her* to be happy, but I still feel a tinge of betrayal whenever I find *myself* bonding with Drew. A conundrum only decades of therapy could unravel. For now, I'll just put the lid back on the box and stuff it deep into the corner of my brain.

Chapter Three

Aubrey

This morning, Cal and I ate cereal together in the kitchen, but neither of us really talked. It's been three days since he dropped that little bomb—telling me my mother decided to tell him he's moving—and then, a few hours later, I got that email. *They have to be connected, right?*

After Sienna's death, my mom changed. I was still young, but old enough to notice that her behavior wasn't normal. Her grief consumed her, transforming her into someone I hardly recognized. Ever since, navigating her unpredictable moods has been a constant battle. She moved us out of Central Oregon and up to Tacoma, claiming everything there reminded her of Sienna.

I never truly understood it. I wanted to cling to those memories—the comfort they could bring—especially with Cal growing up without his mom. But I was also grieving, trying to make sense of everything while suddenly caring for an infant. My world had shifted in ways I couldn't control.

My mom landed a new full-time job, and I had a month before starting high school in a completely new city. *But I just couldn't.* Instead, I begged my mom to let me stay home, doing online classes until I earned my GED. She'd never outright say it, but over the years, her comments lingered—little jabs about what I should be doing with my life: "What about a real job?" she'd ask, as if what I'd accomplished meant nothing. *But she didn't see what I'd built on my own.*

Over the past five years, I poured my heart into a true-crime podcast I started. It took off more than I ever expected—dedicated followers, sponsors, a platform I never imagined I'd have. I've worked tirelessly, sometimes late into the night, chasing stories, editing episodes, building something from nothing. And despite not finishing high school, I have achievements I'm proud of—achievements she can't seem to acknowledge. *Is that why she's taking Cal? Could it be as simple as she doesn't think I'm a good influence for him?*

The self doubt has been pouring in to me like a leaky kitchen faucet. I don't know if it's me, or her, or Cal, that has her suddenly wanting to change everything. *Yet, that email.* I keep going back to the email, the timing of it all, and the gnawing sense that I'm missing something. *One email—is that enough to change my perspective on my own mother?*

Apparently so, and that's how I find myself searching through the condo we've called home since we moved here. It's a spacious three-bedroom, with breathtaking panoramic views of Mount Rainier and the shimmering waters of the Puget Sound. The luxury of having a surgeon for a dad, and a mom who knows how to find ruthless lawyers. *Ruthless lawyers—or (maybe) corrupt ones.*

My mom's room is the main bedroom—pristine and carefully organized, just like the rest of the house. Her closet is a display of perfection, each item neatly hung or folded, no clutter in sight.

I scan the racks of designer clothes, wondering how we

could be so opposite. Her with her orderly, disciplined life; me with my chaotic emotions. It's like we're from different worlds, even though we share the same blood.

Just as I'm about to turn off the light, ready to give up, something catches my eye. Tucked under a pile of shoeboxes, I spot a slightly larger-than-the-rest, black-and-gold custom box. It looks familiar—similar to the others, but this one doesn't have a see-through front.

Curious, I pull it out, holding the box gingerly as if it has a live grenade in it—rather than what could be merely another pair of fancy shoes.

Instead of shoes, though, I find four neatly organized manila folders, all but one labeled: Marriage/Divorce Decree, Birth Records, Sienna's Medical Records—and the last, untitled, sitting at the bottom.

I flip through the first folder, but nothing unusual catches my eye—it's all straightforward, just documents related to my mom and dad. The same goes for the birth records—my birth certificate, Sienna's, hers, and Cal's. I focus on Cal's birth certificate, searching for anything out of the ordinary, but everything looks normal. Rosa Dubrow is listed as the mother, which I assume is because Sienna died shortly after childbirth. *Right?* My eyes drift to the father's field—completely blank. No surprise there, but I can't shake the feeling that Sienna would be upset if she knew Levi wasn't listed. *Even if he is a deadbeat —she loved him.*

Then I notice the hospital information: it says Cal was born at Riverbend. *That's wrong.* He was born at St. Charles, not Riverbend. I know this for a fact—I went to that hospital every day, stared at the logo so often the image is burned into my mind. *So, what does this discrepancy mean?*

"Aunnie! Where are you?" Cal's shout makes me jump, like I was just caught doing something I definitely shouldn't be

—*which, okay, I was.* I carefully set the folders back in place, closing the lid and returning everything to exactly how it was.

"Aunnie!!" he yells again.

"Coming!" I call back, grabbing a random shoebox from the top pile.

When I step out of her closet, he's standing in her doorway with raised eyebrows. "Bruh."

"What?"

"I've been trying to find you everywhere! What are you doing?"

I hold out the box, peering down at the transparent window revealing a pair of black Louboutins.

"Research. Woman killed her husband with a pair like these..." I wave my hand in a stabbing motion.

"Bet," he says, unfazed. "I'm hungry. When can we start lunch?"

"Right now," I say hurriedly, stepping around him and heading toward the kitchen. "What are you craving? We've got leftover spaghetti!"

Why do I sound like I just ran a marathon?

He shrugs. "Cool."

Later, I settle back onto the couch in the living room, my laptop balanced on my lap. I should be working—researching my next case—but I'm stuck on that birth certificate with the wrong hospital. *Is it weird that my mom's listed as his mother?* The question lingers, but I don't know much about adoption laws, so maybe it's normal. *What about Levi not being listed? Does he even know he has a son?*

I mean, he knows Sienna was pregnant... but does he know Cal is his?

Sienna always spoke highly of Levi. I only met him briefly —a quick hello on my way to a friend's house. I never got the vibe he was a loser. Young, maybe a little wild, but not the kind to bail on his pregnant girlfriend. She was happy, nervous about becoming a mom, but she told me Levi seemed happy too—that he'd always wanted a big family.

I try to remember more, but I was so caught up in my own world back then. That summer, we barely saw each other. She'd moved out, mom and her were always fighting, but every once in a while, she'd pick me up for lunch and we would catch up.

Then everything changed when I received the call from Colleen, one of the nurses my mom was friends with.

It was late—almost dark—and Colleen told me Sienna was in the hospital. Without thinking, I biked the three miles there—something I'm pretty sure, if my mom was coherent enough to notice, would've earned me a grounding.

When I arrived, my mom was a mess. I stood in the entryway, right next to the sliding door, watching her scream at Levi. His back was to me, but I could see it on his posture—her words hitting him hard. "It's all your fault! You fucking killed her!" She was so furious that it took three security guards to hold her back and calm her down. Meanwhile, Levi just stood there, enduring it, listening to her berate him like he really did kill Sienna.

But he didn't.

I know that because as soon as he walked past me, I sprinted to the nearest stairwell. I climbed the stairs as fast as I could, only to collapse in a heap on the third floor. A doctor found me there—Doctor Beach. She wasn't one of Sienna's doctors, but she had heard what happened.

I remember her name because her hair was soft blonde, worn down, contrasting against her light blue scrubs. I thought her last name suited her—she looked like the beach: beautiful, warm, and calming.

"Oh my god, are you—?" she starts to ask as she rushes up the stairs, but as she got closer, it was like she instantly recognized me. "Oh, you're—" she hesitated, taking a steadying breath. "Are you Rosa's daughter?"

I nodded, tears spilling down my face, unable to speak or even feel embarrassed that I was crying alone.

Instead of asking more, she sat beside me, and I saw her head bow as her hands clasped together like she was praying. She stayed quiet, searching for what to say.

"He killed her? He really killed her?" *Them.* I turn, still in disbelief.

Her shoulders go straight, and her eyes snap to mine, shock etched on her face.

"Oh, honey, no—no, no. Levi did not kill her. She's not— It's still early, and many tests are still to come. Something caused Sienna to suffer a pulmonary embolism," she explains gently. "She had a significant drop in blood pressure and oxygen supply, leading to widespread hypoxia. Essentially, imagine a tiny blood clot breaking loose and floating all the way to her lungs, where it gets stuck and blocks normal blood flow. This impairs gas exchange significantly. Her brain wasn't getting the oxygen it needed to survive."

"What could have caused that?"

"I don't know for sure... but her doctor suspects that her continued use of birth control pills during the first half of her pregnancy, stress from work and school... or she could've just been predisposed with a clotting disorder. It's hard to say exactly what triggered it. But I can tell you—Levi isn't to blame. Neither is the baby."

"The baby?"

Her expression softens once again, and I notice her shoulders slump, as if she's unsure of what to say. "I think we should go see Sienna's doctor."

"No—please! Just tell me."

"They have her in an induced coma. Like I said, the next few days are critical. The baby is still doing okay; Sienna is hooked up to machines keeping her alive. Whether she'll wake up or not—I don't know. But as of now, no one is dead."

Then why did my mom go off the rails with Levi? And why did Levi just leave?

I'll never forget the security guards holding my mother back as Levi turned and walked away. Or her screaming face, broken and wild. I don't know what was said between them—if Levi said something to set her off, or if she was just projecting her grief. But I'll never forget how her heart looked broken in two, how she grieved her oldest daughter. Honestly, that look never really left her—though maybe that's the Botox and fillers keeping her in a perpetual resting bitch face.

But what about Levi? I close my eyes, trying to picture his face as he passed by me—yet I can't. Maybe I didn't look, or maybe I was crying too hard to see him properly.

My mom never forgave him after that. And honestly, I've struggled with it, too—struggled to forgive him for walking away, for leaving her to face everything alone. *But did he?*

Did Levi, the guy Sienna swore would step up as a good dad to Cal, really just leave her there? Or did my mom say something that drove him away?

It takes me a while to snap out of my derailed thoughts, but when I do, a strange sense of urgency replaces the dread—like I need to know everything about Levi, right this second. I shouldn't be surprised. That's what I love most about podcasting—the research, the hours spent digging into a case, piecing together every detail. It's like my brain craves it.

I type "Levi, Three Sisters Oregon" into Google, and hundreds of articles flood through. The first is a photo, and I recognize him immediately—he's older, but he's wearing a paramedic uniform, standing in front of the fire station. *Levi Turner.* The Turners—Cal's paternal side.

I open a new tab and start reading an older article from The Oregonian, a respected newspaper in the state. It's an anniversary piece about the murder of a sheriff's deputy—Dan Turner, Cal's uncle.

The more I read, the more heartbreaking it becomes. There are photos from the funeral procession—thousands of police officers lining the streets to honor him. I see images of his young kids clutching their mom tightly, tears streaming down their faces. His grieving wife, and two men with hands on her shoulders, supporting her—are Levi, Dan's twin brother, and what appears to be their father, Ezekiel. The resemblance to Cal hits me hard enough to bring tears to my eyes.

The next photo is of Dan's headstone, taken at the funeral. It features a large black-and-white portrait of him in uniform, next to a bigger, colored version of the same image. Red, white, and blue flowers decorate the stone, and behind it, an American flag flies proudly. It hits me in the chest, and I feel my breath catch—this was a man dedicated to serving and protecting, a life cut too short.

"Is that him? My dad?" I'm so lost in the moment that I don't even notice Cal approaching.

Gasping, I turn to find him standing behind me, wide eyes filled with sadness and confusion.

I glance back at the photo, tears already blurring my vision as I'm left speechless.

"It—no..."

"Don't lie, Aunnie!" His voice cracks on the nickname he's used for me since he was a toddler—when he couldn't say "Aunt Aubrey." It slices through me, raw and sharp.

I take a shaky breath, struggling to speak. "Cal, I swear to you. That's not your dad. That was his twin brother, Dan."

He stares at the photo, processing it. "I didn't know he was a twin. We don't—" he hesitates, eyes dropping to the ground, then looks back up at me, sorrow darkening his face. "Grandma said we're not supposed to talk about that side."

I clear my throat. "Grandma was trying to protect you from being hurt. I think she believed if we didn't talk about them, maybe there wouldn't be so much pain."

He nods slowly. "Because they didn't want me?" His voice is barely above a whisper. *God, I could burn the world down for making him feel this way.*

"No, sweetheart. It's not that. That's one thing your mom told me when she found out she was pregnant with you. She said your dad was nervous, but excited. He loved you, Cal—more than you'll ever know. Come sit with me for a second, okay?"

He cautiously slides beside me, still fixating on the photo of Dan.

I subtly scroll back up through the pictures, moving to the family photo before it.

Cal's jaw drops slightly as he takes in the image.

"That's your dad," I say softly, pointing at Levi. He may look older now, but he's still as devastatingly handsome as I remember. "And that's your aunt—her name's Olivia. The kids—your cousins—are Ben and Ellie. This picture was taken a few years ago, so I'd guess they're about six and ten now."

His eyes widen with curiosity. "And that guy is... my grandpa?"

I nod, my gaze drifting to him in the photo. "His name's Ezekiel. He was the sheriff of Three Sisters."

"Are there more photos of my dad?" Cal asks, resting his head on my shoulder.

I set my head on his, smiling softly. "There are thousands. He's—well, he seems to be quite the charmer of the town they live in. That's probably where you get it."

Cal scoffs and shakes his head. "I doubt it," he mutters. "But I do think I look a lot like him."

"That's a good thing," I say gently. "They're all beautiful people."

I hit the back arrow on the browser, bringing up a page filled with dozens of articles about paramedic Levi Turner. My stomach tightens as I scroll through the flood of words, images, and memories.

Suddenly, my eyes catch on a photo—Levi at a charity event, dressed in a ridiculous hot dog costume, grinning like he's having the time of his life.

"He seems... fun," Cal says with a quip before being quiet for a time. "I wish I knew the real reason he wasn't around..." His voice cracks with a mix of anger and sadness.

My chest physically aches for him—the pain of rejection, those unanswered questions. Levi's absence weighs heavily not just on Cal's heart but on mine as well. *Why was he so amazing to Sienna when she was healthy, but the moment things got hard, he bailed? Did he ever care about Cal or was it a facade he put on for Sienna?* The thought of Levi leaving his son, abandoning Cal when he needed him most, fuels a quiet fury inside me. He needs answers—I need answers—and if I have to confront Levi, I will. Cal deserves to know the truth.

I glance at Cal, a surge of protectiveness and resolve rising inside me. *What's stopping us from finding out?* He is almost twelve and is now facing the real possibility that my mother may change his life forever with a move across the country. *A move that takes him away from me.*

She's been ignoring my calls, only responding with vague texts about working overtime. What's stopping us from taking a little five-hour road trip—to see whether Levi is the asshole my mother said he was, or the loving one Sienna described? Nothing.

I text Molly once again; she's been my sounding board throughout this, and it seems like she's been on the same page as me.

Molly Wick

> How detrimental to Cal's mental health would it be if I planned a "let's go meet your dad" road trip?

> Does Cal know beforehand?

> Yes. I'll let him be the final decision-maker, but I figured I should run it by another adult to make sure I'm not losing my mind.

> AND YOU CHOSE ME? I'm just as crazy as you are. I say if Cal is in, then go. Take that boy to meet his (hunk) of a dad, and see if he's as goody-two-shoes as the internet says he is.

Okay, so maybe I mentioned Levi's name just so she could do her own snooping too.

> Glad you're as crazy as me! No school on Friday, which makes this the perfect weekend to go—if Cals wants to, that is. Will send pics!

> YOU GOT THIS.

I'm not feeling as confident as she is, but my options feel even less. *It has to be time, right?* Time to find out why Levi turned away, why he walked out of Cal's life, and what really happened. Time to figure out what has my mom making these rash decisions, why someone is investigating a law firm she used, and why I've been left in the dark. It's time for closure—not only for me, but for Cal. And I have a feeling, the answers to those questions may be the same—and I may just find them in the same place—*Three Sisters*.

Chapter Four

Aubrey

The open road stretched endlessly before us as I eased my Volkswagen Tiguan onto the highway, a surge of satisfaction flooding through me. From the moment I saw this car, I knew it was meant for this—trip after trip with Cal, chasing new adventures, and making memories that Sienna would have been proud of. But really, it's more than just a vehicle; it was my first big girl purchase—my symbol of all the hard work I'd poured in. Paying for it outright with money I earned from the podcast—cash, no loans—made the victory even sweeter, even if my mom seemed indifferent.

This morning, I had packed the car to the brim with every road trip snack Cal could dream of—jerky, trail mix, gummy bears, and even a box of donuts. It was about a five-hour drive, and though we weren't racing against time, the nerves still gnawed at me. *Is this the right decision for Cal? Is Levi going to be a complete douche and ruin Cal's future?* I've talked myself in and out of this trip nearly a dozen times, but I've always come back to the same thought—Cal deserves to know for good what his biological dad is like. If it bites me in the ass, it bites me in the ass, but at least Cal will know. *And he'll go right into therapy.*

I quickly send a selfie of Cal and I, with all our snacks in the background to Molly. She sends about a dozen heart emojis back with a "Bye-buddy! Hope you find your dad" gif that has Cal cracking up next to me.

The engine hummed steadily as I cruised past lush green landscapes, wildflowers—yellow and orange—scattering the rolling hills. Cal sat beside me, strumming along to his playlist—first Billie Eilish, then switching abruptly to some indie band I'd never heard of. The speakers vibrated with the music, and I couldn't help but smile at how much he loved to take control of the stereo. He's no longer a little kid—in stature or attitude.

"I can't believe how fast the school year flew by," I said, glancing over at him. "It feels like yesterday you were all nervous about your first day of sixth grade..."

Cal nodded vaguely, eyes lazily fixed on the window, shoulders slumped. "Yep..." he muttered, voice flat. He leaned back in his seat, eyes drifting over the scenery—a patchwork of forests, distant mountains, and small towns with signs that looked like they hadn't been updated in decades. The mountains in the distance appeared almost dreamlike, as if sketched with pastel pencils, but he hardly seemed to notice.

My gaze drifted to the tattoo on my arm—every time I saw it, I was reminded of Sienna. The vibrant autumn tree, with fiery reds, oranges, and yellows, seemed to dance in the breeze, just like her spirit always did. One branch cradled a tiny nest, holding a single baby bird—symbolizing Cal. Below, the dates etched into my skin mark his birth and the day we lost Sienna. It's my favorite tattoo, and that's saying a lot considering both arms are nearly sleeved—along with a few others on my torso and thighs.

Cal's hand drummed impatiently on his thigh, faster and

faster, matching the beat of the music. Finally, he turned to me, his eyebrows knitting together. "I don't want to move to Florida. It's too hot all the time and there are so many bugs!" His voice clipped and edged with irritation, eyes narrowing as if expecting me to say something to fix it.

I nodded in agreement, shoulders tightening slightly. "Don't blame ya, those bugs were Jurassic Park size."

"I don't understand why I can't just live with you. Grandma's never around anyway."

"I wish you could," I said softly, voice steady.

He looked away for a moment, then challenged, "Then why can't I?" his brow furrowing, frustration and stubbornness flickering across his face.

"To be honest, I don't fully understand her decision to move either—not that I love Tacoma, but..." I hesitated, "Florida just doesn't seem like our speed."

Wryly, he mumbled, "Seems like Grandma's..."

Yeah, kid, it does.

If there's any place my mom would thrive besides Orange County, it's Miami. She lives for the glitz and glam—and while I can appreciate designer bags as much as the next girl, I prefer a more laid-back vibe.

"Are you thinking of moving somewhere else?" he asks after a moment.

"Maybe someday. Unfortunately, I don't have many answers right now." I paused, voice softer. "I'm taking this day-by-day—and even that feels overwhelming. Grandma really threw a wrench into everything, and I'm just trying to figure out where I fit." Truthfully, I'd been thinking about moving a lot because Tacoma didn't exactly seem like our speed either.

My eyes stayed on the road, but my mind drifted to the conversation I had with my mom yesterday. She was calm and loving as she laid out her grand plan, making it seem so reasonable I almost believed her. She's keeping the condo, so I'd be able to spread my wings, live my life—without the constant worry of taking care of a kid. *But I don't want that.* I may not be Cal's mother, but I'm his aunt—the one who's been there since day one.

She made it sound like Tacoma was the place for me, the right path, all the things I should be doing.

Yet, a fleeting thought of finding a place in Three Sisters flickered through my mind. *Would I like living in a small town?* I loved the time we spent in Central Oregon—the weather, the people. But I quickly dismissed the idea. Just reading articles about small-town life didn't mean I was truly prepared for it.

"Hey," I finally said as we turned onto the final highway out of Redmond, breaking the silence. "I found Levi's address online." According to Zillow, he bought a modest two-bedroom with a few acres about six years ago.

Cal raised an eyebrow. "Podcasters can find out anything in a few hours, huh?"

"Minutes, sometimes," I grin mischievously. "It's like being a private investigator—but with a mic and a laptop."

"And your plan is to just show up unannounced and say, 'Hey, this is your kid; why are you such a deadbeat?'"

My jaw dropped, but I couldn't help but laugh at his sarcastic tone. "No, of course not," I said, shaking my head. "I just want to see him face-to-face—maybe get some answers."

He looked at me, concern flickering in his eyes. "What if he doesn't want to meet me?"

"Then I'll call him a deadbeat AND a loser," I say with a shrug, trying to sound more confident than I feel.

He chuckles softly, but I still catch the hesitancy lingering on his face.

"Cal, anyone who doesn't want you in their life is the one missing out, not you," I reassure him, hoping to lift his spirits.

"You're the best kid I know, and if he's not willing to see that, then he doesn't deserve to be in yours."

"I'm the only kid you know..." he says with a hint of a smile.

"Nuh-uh! I know plenty of kids, but you're the best one by far," I reply with a grin.

"Whatever, Aunnie."

The road ahead begins to wind down, crossing a river where people float lazily on inner tubes. Others are standing outside their cars, wide smiles and laughing. I never spent much time outside of Bend when we lived here—aside from the occasional drive to Redmond airport—but the scenery is familiar, and it fills me with a sense of peace. Memories flood back, making me grateful for this moment of nostalgia. It's as if I can almost feel Sienna again, see her in the rushing river and in the smiling faces of those enjoying the outdoors.

"You know, your mom used to love floating the river when we lived here," I say softly. "She took me almost every day that first summer. I was probably about your age." The thought stops me in my tracks—I wasn't much older than Cal is now when she died, but I still had fourteen years with her. And he has none. I'd give anything for him to experience just a little bit of her light.

"Like in a raft?"

I chuckle. "More like an inner tube or pool floaty. I think people paddle-board now, though. Like we did when Grandma took us to Maui."

"That was fun! Can we do it while we're here?"

"Maybe. The water's probably still cold, and I'm not exactly sure what this weekend has in store." If Levi turns out to be the asshole my mom claims him to be, I'll be hightailing it with Cal straight to Bend. I'll show him where Sienna lived and her favorite things. But if things go smoothly, I might just want to stay in Three Sisters. I've spent the last week immersed in articles about the tiny town that was mostly known for its rodeo and stunning scenery—curious if the reality lives up to the hype.

We pass through the high desert plains, and I point out the sagebrush and juniper trees lining the road.

"It's very... brown," Cal observes, looking out the window with a raised eyebrow, and I can't help but laugh. I thought the same thing when I was his age.

"Out here, yes," I say with a grin. "But just wait until you see the sunsets over the mountains—that's when it really comes alive. The colors reflecting off the snow-capped peaks are unreal."

"So, now's kind of decision time," I announce as we begin to approach the Cascadia County line. "Do you want to go meet Levi first thing, or wait until tomorrow?" It's a little after lunch, and I honestly have no idea if he's working or not. I didn't really have a plan other than to find his address and show up.

Cal pauses for a moment. "You're sure he's home?"

"Not at all," I admit. "But we could do a quick drive-by, get a feel for it."

"Okay. If he's there, let's do it. If not..."

"We'll explore town, find a hotel, and check in."

I change the address, plugging in Levi's address, and the GPS routes us. It's only eleven minutes away, but by the looks of it, we have to take a few back roads to get there. Not exactly the drive-by suburban area I was hoping for.

My heart starts to pound as we approach the house, unsure of how this is going to go down. Then, as if luck suddenly took one look at me and dipped, we turn onto the final road—and I realize, a little too late, that it's a dead-end. Instantly, the nerves settle, knowing there's no sneaking out unnoticed if he's home. Even Cal sends me a nervous glance as if he's trying to not say, "oh, fuck."

As we approach Levi's driveway, I take off my sunglasses and turn the music down, hoping that will help me see and hear better—but it doesn't. The driveway is relatively short, with a large silver Duramax pickup truck sitting in it. The house is cuter than the pictures on Zillow—like he's added a big new section to the original structure. There's a wide porch at the front, complete with outdoor furniture, perfect for relaxing in the evenings. Flowers spill out of hanging baskets, adding splashes of color to the exterior. It all feels surprisingly domestic for a single man in his early thirties. For a moment, I wonder if I have the wrong place, then another thought hits—*what if he has another family, and we're about to drop a bombshell on not only him but his wife and potential kids?*

My mind races with possibilities as I finally put the car in park, turning it off. *I really hope I'm doing the right thing here, Sienna.*

"Maybe, wait in the car for a second? I'll go knock," I suggest softly.

Cal nods in agreement, clearly unsure of what to expect.

Taking a deep breath, I step out of the car, trying to brace myself for whatever's coming. Each step toward the shadowed porch feels longer than it should be, and I instantly regret taking my sunglasses off.

Right as I'm about to step onto the porch, the front door swings open. A tall blonde man steps out, turning to lock it behind him as if he didn't see me approaching.

I nervously glance back at Cal, who's wide-eyed and staring at the man in disbelief.

"Uhm, hi!" I call out awkwardly, trying to break the silence.

Levi spins around on his heel, his right hand moving so fast to his hip that I can only stare. There's a gun sitting plainly on his belt, his hand hovering over it.

"Can I help you?" Levi's deep, authoritative voice sounds—

unexpectedly older than I imagined. I look up to see a face I recognize from pictures. Only it isn't Levi—*it's his dad.*

"Yes, sir. I—uh..."

His hand lowers slightly as I fumble over my words, instinctively raising my hands in surrender. Despite the tattoos on display, my piercings, and the defiant look I probably give off, he reads the situation clearly and seems to realize I'm not a threat.

"You must be looking for my son," he says with a warm chuckle, a gentle smile breaking through his stern expression. "He's not off work for a few more hours. I was just dropping off some dinner and watering the flowers—since he's finishing a 48-hour shift."

A wave of relief washes over me, along with a twinge of disappointment. *He's not here.*

When I don't respond right away, he tilts his head, narrowing his eyes slightly. "Something goin' on?" he asks, suspicion creeping into his voice.

Suddenly, I hear the passenger door open. Quietly I gasp as Levi's dad's gaze snaps over, and I see him immediately recognize Cal. His eyes flick from me to Cal and back again.

The tension in the air seems to thicken as Cal steps up beside me, taller than I am but still shorter than his grandfather.

Then, in the calmest move possible, Cal extends his hand and introduces himself politely. "Hello, my name's Cal."

Whether it's the way he says it, or merely his presence, I see Ezekiel's eyes widen—a fraction—and he gives a slight nod, then looks to me.

"I'm Aubrey," I say awkwardly, waving with one hand.

He swallows hard, and for a moment, it looks like tears might be forming behind his eyes. Then he blinks them away and his entire expression morphs into what could only be described as wonder.

"Ezekiel Turner. Friends call me Zeke, but family calls me Pops. You can decide which one feels right," he says softly, his voice warm but steady.

Cal and I exchange a quick glance, feeling the weight behind Zeke's words. The significance of his nickname hangs in the air—*how could Levi have bailed on his own child when his dad is this welcoming?*

"Why don't you two have a seat? I'll grab some sodas from Vi's fridge. I have a feeling there's a lot we need to talk about," Zeke adds kindly.

Chapter Five

Levi

I couldn't help but slump in the passenger seat of the ambulance as my partner Bill drove us toward the next call. My eyes felt heavy as I neared the end of my shift—but, of course, just before the clock runs out, we get one more call.

Normally, I'd be prepping, thinking about the call, communicating with dispatch, but all I can focus on is getting home, sleeping, and maybe catching up on chores. *Shit.* Not maybe—definitely chores. Olivia's hanging flower baskets sit in the front yard, mocking me with their bright colors and endless watering needs. Every spring, they arrived with her big smile, and every spring, they became a nuisance. Now that summer's nearly here and the dry, hot weather is looming, they demand more attention than I'm willing to give. But she loves them, so I keep telling myself to suck it the hell up.

Bill, one of my best friends, is mid-fifties and always the steady hand on the wheel, glanced over as he navigated the busy streets. The weekends here are always lively with tourists flooding in from all over, and while most days I don't mind it, today I'm exhausted by the influx of people.

"Think Loretta's really having a heart attack this time?" Bill asks, side-eyeing me.

I let out a sardonic laugh, chuckling as I watch the street roll by. "Not a chance. Last shift, she called three times while they were on." She's definitely the poster child for the Frequent Utilizers of City Emergency Response Services—we have a term for them, an acronym really, though I'd never call her it to her face or admit it outside of my head.

"Crazy old bat."

"Remember when she really did have a bat in her kitchen, though?"

"How could I forget? She swore up and down she was bitten and asked me to give her the full PEP series—as if I'm a doctor who knows rabies inside out or anything more than the basics of post-exposure treatment." I'm right there with him, knowing the usual protocol she'd be expected to follow, but my license only covers standing orders and approved protocols— basically, we can't prescribe or give her anything beyond what's permitted without a doctor's orders. *And we couldn't even confirm whether she had actually been bitten.*

I glance at the clock on the dash—still two hours until the shift ends—and I heavily sigh. I'm not physically tired, but mentally I feel drained. Our case load was light, yet it felt like I was filling out patient care report forms for hours.

When we finally pull up to Loretta's modest yellow house, the porch light flickers, and I can't help but groan. *Please let this be as simple as opening another jar.*

I radio into dispatch, letting them know we've arrived before I get out to follow Bill. He already has his bag slung over his shoulder and is about to knock when the door swings open.

"Oh! Hello, boys! Thank goodness you're here!" Loretta calls out. She's tiny—lean and frail-looking—her face pinched with anxiety. Her hands tremble at her sides, fingers twitching nervously.

"Hi, Ms. Loretta. We heard you're having some trouble with your chest. What can we do for you today?" He asks, studying her.

"It started with this darn fly," she says, her voice trembling. "It's been buzzing around me all morning, and I just can't get rid of it. Then I started feeling this tightness in my chest, my head—well, you know how I get with these things."

I shoot Bill a quick look, as if to say, 'Is this really happening?' He simply relaxes his shoulders and gives me a 'keep calm' nod.

"Can we come in and take a look? Are you feeling short of breath or anything else?" Bill asks, stepping closer.

"Well, yes—and a little dizzy. If I didn't have those fainting spells, I wouldn't have called," Loretta replies, trying to brush it off.

We step inside. Bill guides her gently toward her dining room table, where she usually sits for us to check her vitals. I scan the room—spotting the fly darting near the window. *The sooner that thing's dead, the sooner we're out of here.*

"Any sharp or persistent pain?" Bill asks, keeping his tone professional.

"No, just that tight feeling... and this fluttering in my chest. It's all because of that blasted fly! But you always say, 'Better safe than sorry,' and to call anytime, so of course I called—just in case it's more."

I hide my fatigued yawn with a soft chuckle. Glancing toward the kitchen, I see it's spotless—just as always. Loretta keeps everything immaculately clean. I drift over to the counter, pick up a fly swatter, and stand there, waiting. Bill's got her vitals, and I know he'll keep her calm while I go hunting.

"Blood pressure's a little high, but nothing concerning at the moment. These flies are annoying—I'd probably lose my temper if one was buzzing around my dinner table, too," Bill says, placating her like the seasoned, well-tempered medic he is.

Loretta whines softly, "Oh, dear, I'm just so tired of always feeling so worried. You know, after Oliver died, things just haven't been the same around here."

"We get it," Bill says softly. "This is probably a stress response—anxiety can cause transient hypertension and palpitations. Nothing that needs further treatment right now, but we'll keep a close eye."

I notice the big, juicy fly sitting on the edge of the windowsill. With a quick, loud smack—dead.

Loretta gasps loudly, and I can't help but grin as I turn to her. "Got him!"

The relief on her face almost makes this whole frustrating call worth it. "Levi, Turner—looks like homemade cookies are in your future." *Definitely worth it.*

By the time we finish up, documenting everything in yet another patient care report, I'm only about twenty minutes behind schedule. Not bad, all things considered. I'll be home by 6:30, able to toss together something for dinner—and maybe even water those damn flowers before it gets dark.

The drive home is smooth—the truck I've been driving since I was sixteen hums along steadily. I should probably think about getting a new one, but the only passengers are Ellie and Ben, and they love riding in "Uncle Levi's big truck." *Someday, though, when it doesn't feel like I have to hold on so tightly to the past because everything keeps changing in the blink of an eye.*

I turn onto the dead-end gravel road; my driveway is the only one back here, surrounded by fields owned by local farmers. As soon as I make the turn, I can tell something's off—I see my dad's truck parked in the driveway, with a grey sedan behind it—one I don't recognize.

While I pull into my normal parking spot, I try to see who is on my porch but the only person I can make out is my dad. He's clearly laughing at something someone said, shoulders shaking, but with the sun setting behind the house, I'm blinded from seeing who's sitting across from him.

Opening the creaky door, I slide out and round the front of the truck, my eyes still adjusting to see who my dad is talking to on the porch. Just then, I see someone step off—someone with a shade of hair I recognize immediately.

My feet freeze, dust kicking up as I come to a sudden halt. I focus on her face, trying to figure out which Dubrow it is. She's young, short—lacking the appearance of the she-devil herself— and covered in tattoos. Bright colors peek beneath her sleeve-less shirt and cascade down her arms, and although I refuse to get caught looking, I swear there's one just below the hem of her crop top.

She approaches with a shaky smile, her hand extended. "Hi. I don't know if you remember me."

My voice catches as I shake her hand. "Aubrey." The word slips out more as a breath than a proper response. *This is not the fourteen-year-old girl I remember.*

I sneak a quick glance back at my dad, wondering what the hell he's doing here with Aubrey Dubrow.

Then I force myself to shake off the nerves, trying to regroup. "It's been a while." *Understatement of the year, idiot.*

She's probably twenty-six or twenty-seven now—full-grown, by anyone's standards—and looks nothing like the girl I once knew. Beautiful, but with a sharp edge, like she'd cut you without a second thought. *Maybe there is a touch of Rosa.*

"Twelve years," she confirms, but I catch a flicker of some-thing cross her face—almost guilt.

I nod slowly, waiting for her to say more, to explain why she's here now. The last I heard, her mom had me banned from the hospital while Sienna was there. It took months to sort out with the staff—by then, she was already gone and most of the staff refused to talk to me.

"I think—" She exhales sharply, squaring her shoulders. My body stiffens instinctively, sensing I'm about to take an emotional hit.

"—and I could be totally wrong, and maybe you are a heartless bastard—" I nearly rear back at her bluntness.

"I think my mother may have misled you about what really happened to Sienna. She didn't die—no, wait, she did. But not until over a month after her embolism. And the baby—Cal, your baby—he survived."

Cal.

Your baby.

My baby.

Survived.

That's when I finally notice who's sitting on the porch swing—a preteen boy, staring at me with an intensity that hits me like a punch. He looks almost identical to Dan at that age— me too—but it's more than just resemblance. It's the way he sits, the way he's looking at me, like he's calculating my reaction— like Dan could see inside my head without saying a word. That quiet, piercing gaze—like he's trying to read me, to understand me. And in that moment, everything feels tangled—like I'm looking into a mirror and a ghost at the same time.

Then, suddenly, everything I thought I knew shifts—and yet, somehow, I feel whole again.

I have a son.

And Rosa Dubrow is the reason I had no fucking idea.

56

Chapter Six

Aubrey

By the time Levi's truck rolls down the driveway, Cal and I have been talking to 'Pops' for nearly three hours. We've already eaten the food he brought for Levi, laughed until we cried, and actually shed tears over the fact that Cal is meeting his grandpa. *It's been surreal.* I hated this family for years, convinced they were all the monsters my mother painted them to be, but spend an hour with them, and you realize that's not true. Could I see Zeke being stern and a badass sheriff? Absolutely. But seeing him with Cal, he's warm and loving.

We didn't talk much about Sienna, but there was a moment when Cal excused himself to the restroom. The only thing Zeke said was, "I know what happened that made your mom not trust Levi. But I'm telling you right now—he had no idea Cal was born. He was heartbroken when he thought Sienna died that day at the hospital. Tried everything he could to see her, but your mom had him banned. If you knew the strings I had to pull just to get him allowed back in, you might think less of both of us."

I didn't know what to make of that, or how to respond, so I only nodded. Then I spent the next hour overanalyzing every word. My mom had Levi banned on the day she went into the hospital—that meant Levi had no idea whether she lived or died, or if the baby was born. I keep circling back to the birth certificate—Sienna's name missing, the hospital different. My gut tells me Levi had no idea that my mom tried to keep Sienna alive long enough for her to carry Cal to term. It was barely long enough—only twenty-seven weeks, and then he spent months in an incubator.

The sound of the truck hitting the gravel pulls my attention away. An older, nearly vintage blue truck, rolls down the driveway—and I see clearly that it's Levi. *Here we go.*

"Please, for the love that is all holy, let me handle this. Stay right here, tell Pops about football, and I'll be right back."

I stand quickly, trying to muster some confidence. Sienna was the brave one—the one confident enough to take on the world. Me? I'm the insecure, poor excuse for a substitute, but I'm all Cal has.

I take my first step, watching as Levi rounds the corner of his truck—only to stumble a bit as he takes me in.

He looks like he's seen a ghost, and while I don't look much like Sienna beyond the hair color, I figure that's enough.

Extending my hand as I walk, I plaster on what I hope appears confident but is really just trembling.

"Hi, I'm not sure if you remember me." Of course he remembers me. I'm his dead ex-girlfriend's sister—and he looks like he's about to vomit.

"Aubrey," he barely breathes my name, but it's enough to send goosebumps racing over my arms. He looks shaken—physically, visibly shaken—and I catch him briefly glance toward his dad, then back to me. He quickly recovers, a charming smile forming. "It's been a while." *My fault, well—my mom's fault, but me by proxy.*

"Twelve years," I acknowledge awkwardly.

He nods slowly, silent, as if trying to make sense of everything.

"I think—" I let out a heavy breath, searching for the right words. Sienna was the type to rip off the bandaid—*say it once, say it truthfully, say it with your chest.*

"—and I could be totally wrong, and maybe you are a heartless bastard—" I watch as his eyebrows shoot up, shoulders rolling back as if his hackles are rising right before me.

"I think you've been misled about what really happened to Sienna." He remains still, frozen in time, eyebrows still raised. Anxiety begins to swirl inside me, and before I stop to think, I word vomit, "She didn't die—no, wait, she did. But not until a little over a month after the embolism. And the baby—Cal, your baby—he survived." *Way to bury the lead, Dubrow.*

I watch the brief flicker of emotions cross his face—shock, but more so disbelief. Then, with a slow, trembling breath, he shifts his gaze toward the porch. And in that moment, I hear the sharp inhalation—the kind that shatters silence—as he finally sees his nearly twelve-year-old son for the first time. His face turns utterly white, all the blood draining away as the disbelief vanishes, replaced by raw, unfiltered recognition. The same blonde hair, deep blue eyes, and wiry frame staring back at him.

And I know, with brutal certainty—damn it, I know—just by the anguish carved into his expression that my mother did this. She lied. She robbed him of years with Cal. She's been hiding it all along.

I don't know if I'll ever have it in me to forgive her. Because this isn't just dishonesty toward Levi. It's a curse on Sienna, too.

And most painfully, it's a betrayal to Cal—who deserved to know, who deserved the truth all along.

Cal being the kid that chooses now to be defiant, starts walking down the steps toward us, and when I turn to introduce them, I see Cal is taking the same approach I did—hand already extended, as if he's fully confident in every move he's taking. A small sense of pride fills my chest watching him move.

Levi watches, his face a mixture of awe and shock. If I look hard enough, I swear I'd see his blue eyes deepen—like Cal's do right before he's about to cry.

"Hey, I'm Cal," my brave little nephew—who's not so little anymore—smiles at his dad. His voice sounds a little older, like he's trying to seem more tough than his age.

My eyes swing back to Levi, and I see his throat bob as he fights the urge to swallow hard. His eyes fix on Cal's extended hand, but instead of shaking it like he did with mine, he grips it and pulls Cal into a tight hug. *You did good, Aubbie.* It's not my voice I hear—that's Sienna's whispering in my mind—and that's enough to make tears stream down my face.

After a moment, Levi looks at me over Cal's shoulder, his head nodding slowly. I see him fighting tears, the pleading and gratitude clear in his eyes. He doesn't have to say a word—I see it loud and clear.

Levi slowly pulls back his hands, settling them on Cal's shoulders. The look in his eyes is the only confirmation I'd ever need—that he had no idea he was a dad, and that he would have done anything to be part of Cal's life. He didn't deserve this.

"So, I guess you're my dad," Cal says with a half shrug, breaking the silence. I can't help the strangled laugh that escapes my chest.

Levi absorbs it, a smile growing on his face, and confirms,

"No guessin', son." The emotion thick in his voice, but I can tell he's trying to lighten the tension. "The Turner genes—ain't no messing with 'em."

I glance up at Pops, standing on the first step of the porch, watching us with the same kind of admiration I feel. I never thought I'd be so grateful it was him I ran into first, but having that buffer at the beginning felt like a blessing.

He shakes his head, as if to clear his own emotion, then says, "Hey, Vi. Ran into these two on your porch and, well"—he glances toward Cal and me with one more look that can only be described as wonder—"well—uh, yeah. I've already done my fair share of questioning to get to know my newest grandson. I'm gonna get out of here so you can have a moment."

I step toward him, throwing my arms around his broad shoulders. "Thank you for being so kind to us."

He softens, bending to hug me back. "You're welcome anytime."

Then he turns to Cal and adds, "And you're both family. No need to call—just swing by my place anytime."

"Thanks, Pops," Cal says, and I swear my heart squeezes so tightly I have to rub at my chest, feeling the ache hit me so deep, I nearly sway.

"Sorry about dinner, Vi," Zeke grins. "We ate it all for lunch, but I did water your flowers."

Levi glances between the three of us, his brows knitted together. "Y'all been here long?"

Cal nods. "A few hours."

"Shi—, uh, shoot, I—sorry," he stumbles over his curse and I can't help but smile.

That is, until Cal throws me under the bus, admitting, "Don't worry, Aunnie cusses a lot."

"I do not!" I scoff, attempting to stomp my foot, but since

I'm standing on a mostly dirt patch in my Birkenstocks, I end up covering my feet in dirt.

"See y'all," Zeke says, before setting his hand on Levi's shoulder and squeezing. He whispers something low—so low I can't hear it.

I see Levi nod, then glance back at Cal and me, before gesturing his head toward the porch. "You feel like sitting out here, or I could take you out for dinner?"

Chapter Seven

Levi

Aubrey exchanges a quick glance with Cal, who shrugs in response—an unspoken conversation passing between them—before she says, "Here's good for now, but I don't think either of us would say no to dinner later."

I take the seat my dad just vacated, and they settle onto the porch swing. My forearms rest on my thighs as if I need to lean forward to catch every word. The nerves start to spike now that the shock of discovering I have a son is wearing off.

How many nights had I lain awake, wondering what our kid would look like or who he or she would be? Now he's here, right in front of me, and every emotion crashes into my chest—guilt, love, sadness, amazement, shock—all jumbled together like a raging storm.

Aubrey hesitates, glancing between Cal and me, leaving the silence to hang awkwardly.

"So, I guess I'll start from the beginning," she says, wringing her hands. "Well, as you know, Sienna died —" Out of the corner of my eye, I see Cal flinch, clearly uncomfortable with either talking about his mom or going back that far. I raise my hands slightly, signaling her to pause.

"Can we—can we save that for later?" I ask, swallowing hard as I meet Cal's eyes and see the relief there. "I do want to understand how we got into this mess, but right now..." I trail off.

Right now, I want to focus on Cal. I meet Aubrey's gaze softly and add, "I really just want to learn about Cal."

All I see is relief and maybe a hint of admiration—*on her very pretty face.*

"That's easy," she grins. "Cal's the best kid I know!"

Cal groans beside her and covers his eyes. "Aunnie!"

"I know, I know," she replies, waving her hands.

"Aunnie..." I echo, sharing her nickname. "Short for 'Aunt' and Aubrey?"

Aubrey laughs. "Yeah, baby Cal had a tough time with two words at first."

Images flood my mind—him as a baby, looking just like my childhood photos or even Ben's.

"I like it," I say sincerely. "Ellie and Ben, my niece and nephew, both called me 'I' for about a year. I'm a little disappointed it didn't stick."

"Pops talked about them a lot," Aubrey responds, her warm smile easing the tension.

"Yeah, he's their only biological grandparent around here, so he spoils them rotten." Although other pseudo-grandparents and uncles spoil them too, biological family is hard to come by around here. We're all about made families.

Cal side-eyes Aubrey, and I notice her shoot him a sympathetic look before reaching over and patting his leg.

"What?" I ask, wishing I knew what they're communicating silently.

"I thought I only had one biological grandparent," Cal

admits with a shrug and a hint of sarcasm. "One who actually wanted to be around, anyway."

I glance at Aubrey, noticing her flinch—an ache of only having one parent around echoes in her expression. *Or maybe it's guilt from keeping us away from him for so long.*

"Your mom being the only one around, I take it?" I ask, trying to keep my tone from sounding too harsh.

Obviously, Rosa Dubrow isn't my favorite person in the world, and I've never met the elusive Doctor Dubrow. Sienna was always reserved when talking about her dad—I'd always thought she was disappointed, disappointed that he didn't fight harder for her or Aubrey.

"Yeah," Aubrey answers quietly. "My dad's... not really in the picture." She looks away, out at the fields, but I notice her grip tightening on her upper arm, right over her tree tattoo.

"I'm sorry to hear that," I say gently, turning to Cal. He's staring at his hands, fingers clenched—holding back a flood of feelings. I want to ask more pry, understand, but I hold back, not wanting him to shut down further.

"Pops isn't like that," I say steadily, watching how Cal reacts to my words. "If you're open to it, he'd love to be part of your life—and me, too—in whatever way you want." I leave my words deliberately open-ended, a silent hope behind them. I'd move heaven and earth to bridge this gap, to make up for what was lost. I'd take Cal into my home in a heartbeat, to catch up on missed moments—and maybe Aubrey, too. *Maybe.* The jury's still out on her, but I have a gut feeling she's nothing like her mother.

Cal nods slowly, but I notice hesitation lingering in his eyes—uncertainty, mistrust. I don't blame him. Growing up, he thought I didn't want him—or that I wasn't interested in being part of his life. And now he's meeting someone trying to win his trust—someone offering him the dad he never had.

When I look toward Aubrey, I see her face soften as if a weight has been lifted—like some long-held hope finally found its voice.

"I really appreciate that," she says softly, her tone warm and genuine. "We got that feeling from him too. He was really great hanging out with us for a good while. And it's clear he cares about his family—like the kind of grandpa every kid dreams of, and a dad too."

I nod, but something urges me to open up a little more. "He —uh—it's complicated. My mom died when I was young, and Pops took it pretty hard. He checked out for a while, focused on work. I guess I have that in common with him. After—well, let's just say I've had a lot of reasons to pour myself into my career."

Aubrey listens, her expression soft with understanding. "Having goals during grief is important," she replies gently, her eyes full of empathy. "It's how you keep moving forward."

I nod and turn away, clearing my throat. "When Dan—your uncle—died—" I start again, voice low.

They nod almost in unison, as if they already knew about him.

"Pops told you about Dan?"

Aubrey glances at Cal, who's staring past us, seeming guilty of something.

"Uhm," she admits hesitantly. "Yeah, he mentioned him. But—we also did a deep dive on you before we got here. Do you know how many articles you're in? You're like the town's celebrity or something."

I chuckle awkwardly, feeling a mix of embarrassment and gratitude for their interest. "Small towns and their gossip," I say with a shrug, trying to break the tension.

"Anyway," I continue quietly, "Dan's death was really hard on all of us. It took about a year before we all started feeling normal again. But my dad changed after that. One day, he just up and retired from the department and became Grandpa of the Year. He still bounces between that tough exterior and this softer side now."

Aubrey's smile is sweet—her dimples deepening, her brown eyes bright with affection. I shake the distraction away—this isn't the time to get caught up in her charm.

"Back to you," I say, clearing my throat as I shift focus back to Cal. "When's your birthday?"

"August 16th," Cal responds casually. I try to do quick math—he must've been born early, perhaps around twenty-seven weeks, but that's a question for later.

"Do you like having an end-of-summer birthday?" I ask.

"Yeah," Cal nods. "Last year, Grandma rented a boat at the lake, and I got to bring some friends." A small wave of relief washes over me—unexpected but so welcome. Rosa might have hated me, but it doesn't look like Cal has suffered in any measurable way. If anything he seems to be living a really great life with her and Aubrey.

"So, middle school, right? Where do you live? Not in Bend, I assume?"

"Tacoma," Aubrey responds at the same time Cal chimes in, "I'll be in seventh grade, but Grandma's making a move to Florida."

I see Aubrey's shoulders tense slightly, but her face remains impassive, as if she's trying to pretend everything is fine—either for me or Cal. I'm not sure which.

My gaze flicks back to Cal, who looks more than annoyed. *Definitely for Cal.*

"Why is she making you move?" I ask sharply, almost without thinking.

"Better schools or somethin'," Cal replies sarcastically again, giving another shrug as if to play off his lack of indifference.

"It's complicated," Aubrey adds, her tone weary. "She's already out there, working and settling in to her new house..."

When I don't say anything, she keeps talking, her tone steady. "She's letting Cal finish out the school year here with me and stay most of the summer. But she wants him out there for his birthday."

I glance at Cal. He rolls his eyes, clearly annoyed.

"And you don't want to move?" I press, my voice rough.

"Not to Florida! There's alligators and hurricanes!" Cal exclaims, exasperated. I almost laugh—almost—but catch myself.

"True," I reply, narrowing my eyes slightly. "Never been, but I've heard the mice are giant there as well."

They fall silent for a moment. I turn to Aubrey, noticing her shoulders still tense and her expression look tired.

"I take it you aren't a fan of Florida either?" I ask softly.

She tucks and untucks the same piece of hair, avoiding my gaze before finally saying, "I, uh—I wasn't invited."

My head jerks back in surprise. "Did you ask to go?"

She side-eyes Cal, who's clearly waiting for her answer.

"I did," she admits quietly, then looks back at me. "She said I needed to stay in Tacoma. That's okay, though. We're still holding out hope we can convince her to let Cal stay with me." She winks at him, a flicker of determination in her eyes.

Is that why they're here?

From her fidgeting and shifting, I can sense there's more to her story—but she's not ready to say it. Instead of pressing, I tuck that piece of information away for later. My focus shifts back to questions about Cal, listening for clues about what he's interested in.

Chapter Eight

Levi

An hour later, I'm back in my truck, driving toward town. Cal had opened up more and more with each minute, and I didn't want to leave, but I was starving.

The second my tires hit the pavement, I grab my phone and dial my dad. He answers on the first ring, as if he'd just been sitting there waiting for my call.

"Vi."

"A son. Can you believe it?" I start rambling without thinking, spilling the chaos in my head to the one person I trust most. Sure, we've had our rocky times—moments of distance—but after we lost Dan, it was like everyone agreed we needed to stay close.

"He's awesome, right? I think Ben's going to love hanging out with him—someone to look up to. They're close in age—only two or three years apart."

"Whoa, slow down," Dad cuts in gently, his tone steady but firm.

"Pops, *a son*. He's alive, he's here, and he's mine."

The words leave my mouth like a rush of air, and they hit

me like a ton of bricks. Yes, he's my son, but I have no official claim—no legal footing.

My dad must be already thinking ahead because he says, "Biologically, yes. But there's still a lot to figure out. And you can't just go in guns blazing. We need to think this through—slow down. Did Aubrey tell you about Rosa?"

"A little. They moved to Washington, and Cal's been living with her and Aubrey since Sienna died. She's been a traveling nurse for awhile—"

"Yeah," he says hesitating. "Aubrey mentioned that..."

"What else did she say? Cal looked like he was shutting down any time Rosa was mentioned, so I tried to keep it all light."

I hear the heavy sigh before he admits, "I noticed that, too—I'm not sure, Vi. I'd like to look into it a bit more, though. If you're okay with it, that is."

"I am... but—" I hesitate, weighing my words. "I don't want anyone to know what's going on yet."

Something's off with Rosa's handling of everything. It's not just on a personal level—*that she did this to me*. There's also a legal side to it. *How did she hide a full baby's birth from the records? How did she manage to keep Sienna's death hidden?* Her obituary never mentioned anything about Cal, and I would know—I've read it a hundred times. I mourned it. They never had a funeral, though, not that I would've dared to go. Rosa had no problem badmouthing me all over that hospital—even now, I swear I catch sidelong glances from the staff here and there.

"I'll keep it close to home, but son, the whole town's going to recognize him. There's no denying he looks like one of us." That was my thought, too. That's why I offered to run into town tonight to grab dinner—I didn't want Cal to become the next victim of town gossip.

"I know—I'm only asking for this weekend. I'm trying to

convince them to come back when Cal's finished with school for the summer—told them they could stay with me now, and also if they come back..."

"Good," Dad replies quietly. "That's good."

We both lapse into silence. I watch the traffic whiz by for a moment before I speak again.

"You know I bought that house from Lovey because it was the one I wanted Sienna and Cal to come home to." At first, I was only planning to rent it, and I did. But the longer I lived there, the more I didn't want to leave. They never even stepped foot in it, but I couldn't shake the idea of living in it with them. Eventually, I bought it, added a new wing with more bedrooms and a bigger kitchen.

"I didn't know that. I don't remember much about that time—except for a few days after, when I got the call from Josiah asking if you were okay. You wouldn't talk about it."

"No, not with anyone."

"Not even Dan?" he asks, and I hear the skepticism in his voice—he knows Dan and I had no secrets. Every fear, hope, or terrible thing we did, we confided in each other.

"Dan knew... eventually." When he told me Olivia was pregnant with Ben, I—uh—well, I freaked out.

The memory of that day hits me out of nowhere and I'm thrown back in time.

I wasn't on shift that day and normally I'd be busy catching up on shit, but for whatever reason Dan was there in the back of my mind, twin telepathy or something. I rolled into Maisie's early, grabbing a few of the cronuts she's been obsessed with making. It's close enough to a donut that I can mock Dan with.

He's sitting in his cruiser, parked in the grocery store lot.

Chuckling to myself, I walk over and tap a finger to his window.

Slowly he rolls it down, looking at me with narrowed eyes as if he can already tell.

"Got ya something, asshole."

"No, thanks."

"It's from Maiiiiisie's I sing-song."

"Dammit," he grumbles before glancing at the bag I have. "I don't even care what joke you have, it's worth it for whatever's in the bag."

Before I can even make the joke, he continues saying, "It's actually good timing. I—uh—well I have to tell you something."

"What? Olivia's pregnant?" I say with a snort before taking a bite.

When he doesn't say anything, I choke and cough up cronut. "You're fucking with me."

He glares, annoyed I'd even suggest it.

"You're not fucking with me." My mind instantly goes to images of Sienna laying on her apartment floor, her hand clutching her belly. Then she morphs into Olivia and suddenly I'm picturing everything that happened to Sienna happening to Olivia. Then it morphs into the car accident I was first on scene with a few months ago, a sixth month pregnant woman wasn't wearing her seatbelt and was flung out the driver window and landed in a nearby field. The blood from her head wound had colored her blonde hair into a matted reddish/pink hue. I saw Sienna in her that day, but today it's Olivia.

I'm gasping for air, bent over heaving when Dan finally pulls me out of it.

He gives me a second, his hands on my shoulders, staring into my eyes, and I swear he can read my mind.

"Sienna was pregnant, wasn't she." He knows all about our relationship, he deduced I was there to take her to the hospital, but I never could admit that I was supposed to be a dad.

I nod once, bowing my head.

"We'll make sure that doesn't happen to Olivia." Within a week he had us in every class he could find about maternity medicine, online, in person. It was like he knew I needed to focus on something productive, something that would help.

"Levi," my dad sternly says, snapping me out of the memory I was lost in.

"Sorry, yeah?" I answer, as I drive into town, passing by tourists who are happily enjoying the evening. The sky is dark, but the streets are glowing with soft twinkle lights and warm streetlights.

I was saying, "Rosa worked hard to cover her tracks, so I have a feeling this won't be easy."

"No, dad, nothing ever worth having is though, right?"

"No, it isn't. Whatever you need. I'll keep things quiet until you're ready."

"Thanks," I pause then continue, "Hey, dad,"

"Yeah, son,"

"I'm a dad."

At first, he chuckles softly, but then I hear the raw emotion in his voice when he says, "Yeah, kid, you are. And you're going to be great at it."

We hang up, and I pull into SnowPeak—thankful they're

open late and that they serve some of the best burgers in town. The first person I see when I open the diner door is my favorite server, Sandra. Her face lights up when she sees me, and she motions that she'll be right over to help. I stand by the empty counter, waiting for her, doing my best not to show how antsy I am.

Sandra's been part of this town her whole life—she's the waitress I've known forever, and she's worked at SnowPeak even longer. Her silver hair's always pulled tight into a neat bun she wears like a badge of honor every day. She's no-nonsense, pretty tough, but she loves everyone in this town—me especially.

Two years ago, everything changed when Harold, her husband, started showing signs of Alzheimer's. At first, she didn't want to admit it. Nobody really did. But eventually, it was clear, and everyone noticed—his forgetfulness, the weird stuff he'd do. Then one day, Harold went missing. I still remember the call. I wasn't on duty, but I went into full search mode—rushing out, driving around town—only to find him sitting by a pond, fishing like nothing was wrong. He thought I was my dad, joked that I was too young and that I was there to arrest him on his private property. I didn't do much that day— just sat with him and talked until he was ready to go home.

Ever since then, though, Sandra's put me on a pedestal— throwing in extra fries, a shake here and there—and I can't say I mind one bit. He's still doing okay; I visit him as often as I can, and I've even been able to take him fishing on his good days. They have someone staying with them as a caretaker for now, but I know the worry is still there for Sandra.

Finally, she comes over with the brown paper bag filled to the brim. I practically rip the food out of her hands while throwing my debit card at her.

"Where's the fire, Trouble-Turner?" she teases, a little smile in her eyes.

"Sorry, beautiful! Starving and dead on my feet," I say with a grin. It's not totally a lie—I do feel wiped out. But what I'm really desperate for is to get back to Cal and Aubrey. I'd stay up all night just listening to them talk if I could.

By the time I'm back out to my truck, I can feel the adrenaline starting to hum through my body again.

Cal. My son. Nearly twelve fucking years old.

There's a list of people running through my mind that I want to call and tell the news to, but I also want to keep this close to the vest. What my dad said was right, this could be a custody battle of epic proportions soon and I need to make sure I have all the facts first. Part of me is itching to call my buddy Hayes, though. He started the Elite Forces Security and Contracting company, which Drew eventually became part owner of. They handle a wide range of services—from hired security for events and businesses to private investigations, bodyguard assignments, and even consulting for high-profile clients. Their team is known for their professionalism, discretion, and ability to handle complex, high-stakes situations. They'd look into this for me in a second if I asked, probably for free, but I don't have any real facts yet. I need to talk to Aubrey alone first and see what her side of this is.

Instead of calling him, I make the drive back to my house in silence, not even bothering to turn on the radio. There's so much I need to learn, so much I'm desperate to hear about, but one thought keeps circling in my mind—how to get them to stay.

When I arrive, we eat inside, and barely a moment passes before Cal and Aubrey bombard me with hundreds of questions. They're not just about my family—they delve into our entire friend group, the history, and how we've all become so intricately connected.

By around eleven, I show Cal to one of the guest rooms and Aubrey to another. I expect them both to settle in for the night, but about ten minutes later, I hear soft footsteps walking down the hall.

Aubrey steps out—somehow wearing an even tighter crop top that barely contains her tattoos, along with tiny shorts that expose one leg completely. Tattoos have never really been my thing, but the vivid colors against her olive skin somehow feel like a moth drawn to a flame.

Suddenly, I realize I've been staring so long that I must look like a creep. I quickly look away, but not before I notice the slight quiver of her lip and the flicker of uncertainty in her eyes. Her fingers fidget at her sides, hesitating before she finally speaks.

"My mom's trying to take Cal from me," she says, her voice trembling just enough to reveal her distress. "I don't know why she's cutting me out of his life, but I can feel that there's something going on."

I nod. "Is that why you're here?"

Her shoulders recoil noticeably, then she pulls them back, straightening. "It was the catalyst. Can we sit?" She motions toward the dining room table, and I take the seat across from her.

"Why are you here, Aubrey? It's been almost twelve years." I ask the question that's been burning in my mind since last night. *Why now?*

"Besides my mom trying to move Cal to Florida, I got an email last week—someone's investigating the law firm my mom used to 'legally adopt' Cal. The thing is, I don't think she ever actually 'adopted' him. I think she had a hospital falsify documents to say she was his biological mother."

I stare at her, blinking slowly, trying to keep my composure. Being honest about my feelings about Rosa Dubrow probably wouldn't go over well.

"Okay," I say slowly. Then I ask, "Who was the email from?"

She pulls out her phone, unlocks it, and scrolls until she finds the message.

"L. Lincoln?" she questions, raising an eyebrow like I should know the name, but it doesn't ring any bells.

Then she hands me her phone, and the first thing I see is the sender: LLincoln@EFSC.com. My heartbeat quickens when I notice EFSC and suddenly recognization dawns on me. Lincoln is a friend of mine and also one of Hayes's employees at the company I was thinking about calling earlier.

The next line gives me all the answers I need, without even reading the bulk of the email. Subject: Inquiry Regarding Potential Irregularities—Mitchell and Walton Law Firm.

Motherfucking fuck.

Mitchell and Walton Law Firm was owned by none other than our former Mayor, Cyrus Walton, and his asshole partner Marcus Mitchell. I knew they were under investigation by the FBI, but I hadn't realized Hayes's team was digging around there too. The relief in my chest rises, but it's quick to be replaced by a sense of urgency—time to call him.

"You know him?" Aubrey asks, but it sounds more like a statement than a question.

"I do. He works for Drew and Hayes."

She offers a soft smile. "I had a feeling. Small town. And when I Googled the address, I saw it was in the same building as Olivia's."

My eyebrows raise. "You really did do your due diligence."

"I wanted to know what I was getting myself into," she says, then pauses before adding, "Plus, I saw articles about a woman named Isla working for Olivia, and her dad working at the law firm."

That's barely scratching the surface of the chaos that unfolded last winter.

"Yeah, Isla's great. Her boyfriend's Everett," I say, and she nods along.

"Everett's the pilot?" she asks, and before I can respond, she continues, "And Odessa Astor's brother?"

I nod and laugh. "Yep. Dess is great. You'll love her."

"You call her Dess?!" she gasps, eyes wide. I raise an eyebrow in response.

"She's—she's a literal supermodel. You do know that, right?" she blurts out.

"I do. She's also dating my best friend, Luke."

"Luke—the sheriff who took over for Pops."

"The one and only."

She hesitates, blinking twice quickly—like she's nervous.

"Go ahead, ask," I encourage.

"It's not—it's personal."

"Think this whole day has been pretty damn personal, Aubs," I reply, slipping into her nickname without meaning to, but noting how her smile, with that dimple popping, makes me want to keep it.

"Luke and Dan were partners? Was he there the day Dan died?" The question hangs in the air, and my chest sinks immediately.

"No," I say, glancing away for a second. "Luke was dealing with a different situation that day. His girlfriend at the time was involved in a motor-vehicle accident. He was already at the hospital when we got there, though."

She nods, but then her eyes widen as she gasps and clutches her arm, covering her tattoo as she squeezes. "No—you don't mean..." Unfortunately, I very much do.

"I was on duty when Dan was shot." The one who fought like hell to keep him alive, but it wasn't enough. He died on the way to the hospital, and there was nothing I could do to bring him back.

"Levi—that's..." she pauses, and I try to smile, but it feels tight and hollow.

"Yeah, small town. We knew the risk, working together." I try not to sound curt, but I'm already done with this conversation.

Somehow, it's like she senses that too—reading me like a book and changing the subject. "So, Luke's girlfriend died in the accident, and now he's dating Odessa?"

"Uhm—no." I launch into the story about Maddy and her traumatic brain injury. Then, because I can't seem to stop talking, I share more about Odessa and Luke's relationship and how they recently got back together.

"That's—insane. But also, is it bad of me to say 'Go Odessa'? Like girl power to the max, making him fight for her."

I chuckle. "They still haven't announced it to the town yet, but the rumors are definitely flying."

"I kind of love this little town, and I really haven't seen much of it yet."

"Do you think you'll come back?" I can't help myself from asking.

She sighs and takes a sip. "Guess we need to circle back to the first question you asked."

"When I got that email, everything started clicking into place. The way my mom has always been so protective of Cal— she all but banned me from talking to any of my friends from Oregon. He was born, and the very next day, we were at a hospital in Seattle. She hired movers to pack up our house—I thought it was grief, starting over with an infant. But—"

"But now you think it was a deliberate attempt to isolate

you so no one could ask questions about Sienna," I finish her sentence.

She nods, tears welling up in her eyes. "I don't know. That's the hardest part. I tried to call my dad, but it was always dead on the other end—like he blocked me."

"I tried to call Sienna's phone a few times, just to listen to her voicemail—my number was blocked too." I only know because I used the stations phone one time and it went right though.

"My mom really does love Cal, though. He has everything he could ever want—we have a beautiful condo, he goes to a private school, he has friends..."

My heart squeezes at the thought, happy that he's had a privileged life, but at what cost? Not having a relationship with any of my family—it still stings.

"I thought he was happy," she says softly, "but then he caught me 'doing my due diligence.'"

She pauses, then adds lightly, "He saw the picture of Dan's funeral, and I saw the heartbreak on his face when he thought his dad, the dad he never met, was dead. And I realized right then that he should at least know who you are."

She inhales sharply. "Then we started looking at articles that had you in them, and you just seemed so... charming? Perfect? Kind? I don't know. I just couldn't reconcile the heartless boy who refused to take responsibility for his son but would spend his free time delivering babies in an office."

A half-laugh chokes out of me as I remember the day I helped Charlie and Hayes have their baby August. Of course, the local paper wrote a full feature on it, painting me as a hero when really, I was only doing what I've been trained to do.

"I wouldn't necessarily say I'm any of those things," I admit, "but I also would never have abandoned Cal. I was—" I pause, inhaling sharply, feeling the weight of the memory. "I was excited to be a dad. Sienna and I were new, but I used to imagine having a big family."

"Used to?" she repeats, picking up on my slip.

"My idea of the perfect life shifted when I thought Sienna and Cal had died."

She nods slowly. "I'm sorry—that you thought you lost them both."

"Me too."

"I don't expect you to forgive her—my mom. What she did was horrible, and I have no excuses."

"Good—because I'm not sure I ever could."

I spend the rest of the evening explaining to Aubrey every challenge I faced trying to return to work. There were false reports accusing me of mistakes or misconduct, sent to authorities—rumors that spread like wildfire, questioning my work ethic, competence, and behavior among staff and supervisors. Someone was calling every superior I had, badmouthing me relentlessly, trying to get me blacklisted. If it weren't for my dad's reputation in Central Oregon, I honestly believe I would have been pushed out entirely.

I thought I was over it, that I could finally move on. I convinced myself she was just a grieving mother, whose misplaced anger had been directed at me. But now, knowing she was hiding my own child from me—that's unforgivable. And it changes everything.

Chapter Nine

Aubrey

Laughter in the dining room startles me awake, and I nearly jump out of bed. It takes a solid five seconds for me to remember where I am—Levi's.

Yesterday was... special, sad, unique, unbelievable. There's an endless list of emotions to describe how I felt about Cal meeting Levi for the first time.

The second he saw him, pulled him in for that hug, I knew he had no idea what was coming.

We stayed up late after Cal went to bed, and he explained the hell my mother put him through. I wish I could say I was surprised, but for some reason, I wasn't. My mother has always done whatever she could to come out ahead.

It made me think—made me wonder what she said to my own dad. *Did he bail when things got hard? Or was that just the same lie she told over and over?*

I take my time getting ready this morning, letting Cal and Levi have a little more time to get acquainted. When I step out, I'm greeted by the smell of food being prepared.

"Good morning!" I sing cheerfully.

"Hey, sleepy-head," Levi grins from the other side of the kitchen. He's completely shirtless, wearing loose-fitting grey sweatpants—the kind that women drool over— and it's the first time I realize how ripped he is. His hair is still tousled from sleep, and—*oh shit*—

You cannot have a crush on your dead sister's baby daddy.

You cannot have a crush on your nephew's dad.

You cannot crush on Levi Turner.

"How'd you sleep?" he asks, flipping an egg in the pan, completely unaware of the inner craziness going on in my brain.

"Great!" My voice comes out high-pitched and squeaky.

Shit, get it together, Aubrey.

I've dated, been in long-term relationships, and spent nights with some of them—I shouldn't be acting like a teenage girl with her first high school crush.

"How's it going out here? Smells good," I say more casually.

Cal speaks up first. "Yeah, he's a really a good cook. Not like you and Grandma."

He's not wrong but I at least attempt to take offense to that and huff out, "I can make... stuff."

"Burn stuff, you mean," Cal mutters under his breath, and Levi chuckles before coughing to cover it.

"Who taught you to cook, Levi?" I ask, shifting the focus.

"Comes with working at the station. We all take turns, and you learn quickly so you don't get made fun of."

"What are we doing today?" Levi asks as he sits at the table with his own plate.

"Aunnie wanted to show me some of my mom's favorite places."

Levi nods, chewing slowly, then looks at me almost nervously. "Are you sure you don't mind if I tag along?"

"Not at all. This trip, along with meeting you, was about remembering Sienna."

He swallows hard but then forces a smile. "Old Mill district was her favorite—shopping, floating the river—"

"Aunnie mentioned floating the river!" Cal exclaims excitedly.

"It's freezing right now—" Levi starts, and Cal laughs. "She said that too."

"Maybe next time you come, we can float, but today we'll check out the area. There's this new place where people surf on the waves in the whitewater channel. It's pretty fun to watch."

"Cool!" Cal responds eagerly.

"What about the campus? A lot has changed, but most of the buildings are still the same."

I look at Cal and nod. "The high school she graduated from is on that side of town too," I say, recalling the one I was going to start at before we had to leave.

Levi looks at me. "Do you remember much about living here?"

I nod. "Enough. We lived here for close to three years, and I went through middle school here, so I have a few core memories."

"That's right."

"What else can we see?"

"There was this late-night taco place she loved. They changed their name, but it's basically the same food. And it's terrible! But she tortured me plenty eating there—how about that?"

We finish up breakfast, and I clean while Levi showers. It gives me a chance to really observe his house. It's nice—not a full bachelor pad, but clear he's single and lives here.

He comes out wearing jeans and a tight-fitting short-sleeve shirt, and I quickly glance away.

"Ready?"

I nod, and we all follow him out the door.

"Want to take my car? With all the driving I'm sure it gets better gas mileage."

He chuckles, but I catch the hesitation.

"You drive, though. I'd have to use Google Maps for everything."

If I weren't watching him, I'd miss the way his shoulders relax a fraction. Interesting.

Cal steps off the porch after putting on his sneakers, and I motion for him to sit in the front. "I'll take the back." These two need all the bonding they can get.

He shrugs and climbs into the passenger seat. Levi gets in, adjusting the seat to fit his frame—nearly a foot taller than me—and then he looks into the rearview mirror. Catching me staring, he winks—yes, actually winks—and heat rushes to my cheeks as I quickly look away.

You. Can't. Have. A. Crush. On. Him.

He drives, talking the whole time, asking questions to Cal as if it's the most natural thing in the world. He listens intently, laughing, offering little pieces of advice. I don't know if it's just his natural charm or if being near his niece and nephew plays a role, but he's incredible with Cal. It's hard to believe that yesterday morning I was nearly breaking out in hives, thinking he'd brush Cal off and want nothing to do with him.

He shows us the surfers, and we watch for nearly an hour as three men take turns riding the waves.

"You want to learn?" Levi asks Cal.

Cal's eyes go wide. "You know how?"

"I know the very basics, but we could learn together. I'd be happy to bring you here this summer and put in the work." *Put in the work.* Maybe I'm reading more into it, but it feels like he's promising more—saying more.

I blink quickly, fighting back tears that sting my eyes.

"You know, one time your mom convinced me to go paddle boarding," he says, shaking his head with a laugh. "And I was doing damn fine, keeping my balance, feeling proud of myself—until out of nowhere, she hit me in the butt with her paddle so hard I lost my footing and ended up flat on my back in the water. I couldn't even retaliate because by the time I got it together, she was twenty feet away heading back to the shore."

Sounds just like Sienna—the life of the party, always up for being silly. And that guilt, knowing Levi loved her—so much it's obvious—begins to gnaw even more. Me having a stupid crush? It's just... stupid.

Needing a little space, I hold my phone up, even though the screen isn't lit. "Need to go be on a call." — kind of true, I need to call Molly and give her the latest update on this madness.

She answers on the first ring, sounding sleepy even though it's nearly eleven. I'm guessing, as always, she's a twenty-three-year-old living the LA life—probably up late working on some project or deadline. I usually don't hear from her before noon, but she's always been on top of her work, so I've never minded. She can do her thing whenever, as long as it gets done.

"Molls—" I start, voice a little groggy, a bit whiney. I keep walking away from the guys, toward the other side of the river where a bench for me to sit it. It's far enough away they can't hear me, but still in eye-sight.

"Oh, no," she guesses instantly. "You love him." *And bam, right on target.*

"How on earth could you possibly know that?!"

She laughs, still groggy but a little more alert now. "Because I know you. You don't use that voice unless you're feeling guilty about something you're probably going to do anyway." I look over and see Levi laughing at something Cal says, then pointing back toward the water.

"Well, I absolutely cannot. Not only did he date my sister, but the way he talks about her? He loved her."

"That does make things complicated. Is it just because he's hot? Because that feeling goes away pretty quick, you know. Just look for all his 'icks,' and you'll move on fast."

I let out a heavy sigh, and she's not wrong. I barely know Levi, and after all these crazy emotions—meeting him, seeing him love Cal—it's probably more hormones than anything else. That's what I tell myself, anyway.

"Oh—by the way, I've been meaning to call. You know the Markowski case?" My brain automatically shifts into work mode as I recall the case of a missing eleven year old girl.

"Anything from the aunt?"

We've been waiting to hear back from the girl's aunt to get her side of the story.

"Better—the dad. The accused dad."

"You're joking! What did he say?"

"That he'll only talk to you about it, but he wants to share his side of what happened."

"Ugh—what do we do?" I hate the idea of giving that scum any attention, but on the other hand, he's never actually been charged in her disappearance.

"I don't know, babe. Do you want to think about it and let me know?"

"Yeah, give me a few days. My gut is telling me no though."

The good thing about our podcast is that I can record a few weeks—or even months—ahead of time. That way, I don't stress over deadlines, and I have the space to carefully consider how I want to tell this story.

When I hang up, I notice Levi looking at me, a question in his gaze—like he can feel my energy shift.

Cal, thankfully oblivious to the weight of everything, yells from the bridge, "Aunnie! You ready?"

As I make my way back to them, I try to steel myself, to throw that armor back on, and remind myself—above all—to focus on Cal.

Chapter Ten

Levi

"As terrible as I remembered," I say with a grin as I round the car, climbing back into the driver's seat of Aubrey's car. The relief I felt when she asked me to drive was insurmountable, and honestly, it's also completely irrational. I hate riding with others; it's one of my tics—a habit formed from years of witnessing things most people could never imagine.

As a paramedic, I've seen too much—injuries so severe they haunt your dreams, accident scenes that leave your mind racing, every kind of trauma you can imagine. I've watched people at their worst, and because of that, I don't trust anyone else in the drivers seat. Not when lives are on the line, and not when I have the chance to be in control.

We just finished dinner at the taco place Sienna loved, and I'm already regretting the decision to order the giant Oregon burrito filled with carne asada and grilled potatoes. Cal must be feeling the same—he groans next to me, holding his stomach.

I glance at the dash as I start the car: 07:00. Twenty-four hours ago, I was getting off work, completely unaware that my life was about to flip upside down. Now, I've got a kid—well, a kid I know about—and he's pretty incredible. Funny, respectful, reserved but still full of personality. I see so much of Aubrey in him—little bits of Sienna peek through too—but his sarcasm and wit? All Aubrey.

She's been unexpectedly gentle and patient with him—more than I would have expected, given how loud and bold her appearance is. I've been itching to ask her about her tattoos. They'd be completely hidden if she wore a high neck or long sleeves—almost like it's intentional. I can't help but wonder how Rosa Dubrow, who's so uptight and traditional, feels about her edgy daughter.

Sienna was always a free spirit, but even she wouldn't have gone against her mother and gotten a tattoo. And Aubrey's career? True crime podcaster isn't exactly the most conventional choice. Sienna used to tell me she dreamed of being an artist, but she knew her parents would only support her if she pursued something more stable—becoming a dental hygienist.

I've started noticing the little rebellions Aubrey's been making—her bringing Cal to meet me is probably one of them. Another is the way she dresses—vibrant, confident, unapologetically herself, with outfits that have a touch of boho rock, yet are mostly black.

The back door clicks shut, and I see she's back there again, which means Cal is in the front. I haven't said anything about it, but usually, kids are safest in the backseat until they're thirteen. On the other hand, I know he's big enough—height and weight-wise—to sit up front. I've kept my mouth shut—mostly to avoid rocking the boat—but I'm still being extra vigilant while I drive. I wonder if this is what Hayes was talking about the other day, when he said he drove about ten miles under the speed limit on his way home from the hospital with August. *Precious cargo.*

By the time we get home, it's not late, but everyone looks

exhausted. Cal excuses himself, dragging himself to his room. One damn day, and I already think of it as his room.

I shake the thought aside as Aubrey steps into the dining room. She pours herself a glass of wine, her shoulders turned away from me, and then—with a large gulp—she drinks nearly half before refilling it.

Then she turns to me, eyes locking with mine—somewhere between determination and vulnerability.

"I know we talked about it briefly last night, but I'd like to bring Cal back for the summer so he can get to know you. I have enough saved up to rent—"

"Stay here," I intercept firmly, cutting her off before she can finish.

She swallows hard again but doesn't break eye contact. "One condition."

I nod, listening intently. "You can't make him any promises. I don't know what's going to happen. I don't want him to move to Florida, but I also don't know if moving here is the best answer right now. I'm—I'm a mess. I don't know what to do. I'm making impulsive decisions, driving five hours so Cal can meet a dad he's never even heard about." I try to hide it, but it hurts that he never knew who I was.

"I don't want to hurt Cal in any way," I say softly, "and I promise I'll always do what's best for him. But—do you honestly think that moving to Florida is the best thing for Cal? When you've met me, my dad, and you see that we'll be there for him, no matter what? I'm not saying he has to move here, but if you think for a second that me knowing he exists doesn't change everything—you're wrong. I will fight to be part of Cal's life—in whatever way he wants."

She sighs heavily, then shakily adds, "Can we please just take it slow before calling in the cavalry? Let's talk to your friends when we get back, see what they know. I'll do some digging on my own, and when we come back, you can decide what to do."

"Aubrey—" I reach over and gently place my fingers on her hand. "*We* will decide what's best. You and me—Cal isn't just your nephew. He's as much yours as he is mine. I want you to know—you are just as much a part of this family. Rosa—I don't know about her yet. I still have a lot of anger. But I can also see that Cal was taken care of, and I haven't completely written her off. But you? You righted that wrong yesterday. You brought him to me."

Her eyes glisten, but she quickly blinks them away. "I trust you. I don't trust many people—probably only Cal, and Molly, if I'm honest. But I trusted you the second I saw you with him. Your dad, too. He's—" she pauses before adding softly, "real. And raw. Like you just know he's genuine, that he cares deeply. And that means a lot to me."

"Everyone in my family is like that," I say, voice thick with emotion. I take a shaky breath. "I know I've talked a lot about my friends, but I want you to understand—they are the strongest, most trustworthy people I know. It's not enough to say I trust Hayes and Drew with my life—I trust them with Ben and Ellie's, with Olivia and Charlie's. They're good people. And when you're ready, I know they'll handle this situation—not just with care, but so thoroughly they'll get to the truth of whatever happened. No stone left unturned. And if it comes to a custody battle with Rosa, they'll fight tooth and nail to ensure Cal's happiness and well-being is the top priority."

I watch her pretty little head tilt, and her eyes close as she takes in what I've just said. The wine has already added a rosy hue to her cheeks that I can't help but admire. She's beautiful on the surface, but knowing how much she cares about Cal elevates her to a whole new level.

When she opens her eyes again, they're brimming with

emotion, her voice soft but piercing. "I've spent every day since he was born putting him before my own needs. I've loved him, cherished every second with him, and been grateful for him every single day, Levi. I don't understand why my mom is doing this, but I'm begging you—please don't do the same to me."

My voice catches slightly, thick with emotion and conviction. "I promise you, Aubrey. My opinion—Rosa's, her judgment—be damned. Cal's well-being is what matters most. I would never, ever take him away from you."

For a moment, we just hold each other's gaze—her eyes shimmering with unshed tears, mine filled with resolve. That silence stretches between us, heavy and undeniable. I can't predict what the future might bring, but this I vow: no matter what happens, Cal will always be my first priority. I will fight with everything I have to keep him safe, loved, and surrounded by those who truly care for him—and I know, without a doubt, Aubrey is one of those people.

Chapter Eleven

Aubrey

"You'll love the rodeo, then. It's the biggest event the town has every year, and thousands of people from all over come," I hear Levi say, and pause inside the house with my foot hovering over the step, coffee in one hand.

Levi and Cal are sitting on the front porch, and I can't help but take a moment to listen to their conversation. Cal may be a little reserved, but I can tell he really likes Levi. And Levi has been better than I could have imagined—easygoing yet welcoming, letting Cal open up at his own pace.

I smile to myself, letting the moment settle in. After the conversation Levi and I had last night, I barely slept—tossing and turning, wondering if I'm doing the right thing by keeping my mom out of this. She loves Cal more than anything, and I know she messed up by keeping Levi away. Yet, I can't help but wonder if there's a reason I'm missing. *She's not outright evil, right?*

Still, hearing Cal belly laugh at the way Levi describes Ellie eating too much cotton candy, or groan at some of the injuries Levi's had to deal with on shift—it's the reassurance I needed.

After standing there like a creeper, listening for a few minutes, I finally step out. Both of them look at me.

Levi offers his usual friendly smile, and I can't help but feel a tingle all over my skin. I immediately glance at Cal, who quickly averts his eyes toward the car, and I see his shoulders sag—like seeing me is a reminder that we're going home today.

"Sleepin' the whole day away, Aunnie," Levi teases with his best mockingly annoyed voice, and I roll my eyes, padding my bare feet across the rough wood boards.

"Where are your shoes? You're gonna get slivers!" Levi pops up, brushing past me into the house.

I look down at Cal, who shrugs and lifts his sneakered foot. He's already fully dressed—sweatshirt and jeans—which surprises me. For a kid who usually sleeps until ten on non school days, I'd expect him to still be in pajamas.

I raise an eyebrow. He just shrugs again and explains, "We went for a walk really early. He showed me this cool field with like a hundred elk in it."

"Why didn't you wake me?! I want to see the elk, too!"

He shrugs again. "I only woke up to go pee, but I heard someone in the kitchen."

Levi walks back out, and I notice he's wearing jeans, paired with a tight henley that clings to his frame.

Before I get caught staring, I glance away, but I'm distracted again when he swings my black sandals into view, setting them down in front of me. My jaw drops.

Then, as if that wasn't the nicest thing a man has ever done for me, he plops into the chair across from us.

"What'd I miss?"

"Not much," Cal begins. "Just telling Aunnie about the elk."

Levi grins. "Cool, right? Next time you come, I'll take you over there too."

I smile, feeling a warmth in my chest at the thought of exploring more of this place with—*no, not with Levi,* only more of this beautiful place.

"Love to see it," I say, then quickly look away. "Speaking of which, we should probably hit the road soon. It's a school night, so we don't want to be rolling in too late."

I bump my shoulder into Cal, and he suddenly looks solemn again.

When I glance back at Levi, he has the same sad expression—like they could be twins.

Levi quickly shakes it off, trying to smile, but it looks more forced than genuine.

"Aunnie's right. Don't want to be tired at school tomorrow." Then he looks to me, asking, "You got any big cases you're working on this week?"

My head jerks up toward him, and I stare for a second. Most people—aside from Cal and my team—don't even ask about my podcasting.

"Uh, well—yeah. A few actually. I'm finishing up one from Wisconsin. I had a family reach out about their daughter's disappearance and her ex-boyfriend's potential involvement. It's really sad—the more I dig into it, the worse it gets. Her family's completely tapped out. The ex is from a well-off family and hired the best attorney. The state didn't have enough to convict him, but she's still missing, and I just really want to make sure—" I trail off, realizing I might've said too much.

Levi's eyes soften before he finishes for me, "do it justice."

"Exactly," I nod, relieved that he understands the gravity of the situation. "I just want to raise awareness about her case, even if it doesn't lead to any new answers. Her story is so important, and I want to keep her memory alive in the public eye. It's the least we can do for her and her family."

Levi nods in understanding. "You're doing a good thing, Aubs. It might not seem like much to most, but I guarantee to her family it means the world."

"Yeah," Cal chimes in. "You wouldn't believe how many thank-you letters she's got in her office." I chuckle at the word 'office'—it's really my closet turned into a podcasting room. Before I can say anything, he continues, "She even helped find this kid who was kidnapped by his dad—like five years ago."

I nod, looking back to Levi to explain. "That one was crazy. The dad had weekend visitations, never showed up that Sunday night. He left the country and ended up in Puerto Rico. I had a listener—she saw the age-progression photos and sent me an email. The photo was of her neighbor's son. She said her mom used to babysit him when he was about four, and he kept saying he missed his mom, who lived in 'Brookin'. But the dad denied it, said she'd died."

"You're joking," Levi says, eyes wide with shock.

"Nope. He was trying to say 'Brooklyn,' where they were from."

"Holy shit, Aubrey! What did you do when you got that email?"

"Freaked out! I called like twenty different people trying to get someone to listen. Finally, I got ahold of the officer who was the first on scene. I explained everything—he believed me right away and took it from there. They had him home within a week, and the dad was extradited back to the U.S. and went to prison."

"That's incredible," Levi says, his tone lowering in awe as he gazes at me.

"It was. But I can't take all the credit. My listeners are amazing—they're so supportive. They made it all possible."

"Yeah, but you put in the work too—researching the case, crafting a compelling story that honored the missing child and his mom—and ultimately helping bring him home. That's unheard of," he adds with a smile.

"Thank you," I reply humbly, grateful for the recognition. I believe in calling out the bad in the world, and I want to make it a little better.

He turns to Cal, raising one finger. "Promise I won't kidnap you," then he raises a second finger. "Promise we won't move to Costa Rica."

Cal laughs. "It was Puerto Rico."

Levi's grin falters for a second, then widens. "Exactly," he says, raising his eyebrows mischievously.

I laugh, standing up and turning to Cal, reaching for his hands to pull him up.

"Come on, before you two end up planning some international heist to skip out on moving to Florida."

Levi stands too, still laughing. "Well, we'd definitely avoid Central America. It's basically one giant Florida, but with better food and drinks."

Cal nods eagerly. "Agreed. Canada?"

Levi grins and raise his hand for a high five. "Hell yeah! Maple syrup, hockey, and normal-sized bugs!" *Hot and funny— yeah, I'm totally screwed.*

We spend the next hour packing up our things, which somehow have been strewn across Levi's house. I didn't realize it was so easy to feel "at home" somewhere so quickly, but less than forty-eight hours, and I'm walking around like I've lived here forever. Cal, too, casually heads to the fridge and pours himself a glass of orange juice as if it belongs to him.

It's not the house, though. It's Levi. He's made it feel so natural, like we truly belonged here.

Then the moment comes to leave, and the atmosphere

shifts again. The mood drops, somber and heavy. Cal becomes a little more closed off, retreating inward. Levi tries to put on a brave face, but the optimism doesn't quite land. And me? I'm overwhelmed by guilt—the guilt of once again taking Cal away from Levi, knowing how much he loves him.

As we pull out of the driveway, I catch Levi in the rearview mirror. It's heartbreaking. He loves Cal, and I hate the thought of leaving so soon. But I don't have a choice. There are things we need to address back in Tacoma, and Cal still has to finish school.

Chapter Twelve

Aubrey

Not even five minutes after we get home from Oregon, my cell phone rings — and it's my mom. She's barely called since she left, but the timing of this feels off, and my stomach sinks.

"Hi, Mom," I answer, trying to sound normal but ending up sounding much too chipper.

"Hello, darling! How are you and Cal?" Her voice sounds like she's had at least a bottle of wine, maybe even a few espresso martinis.

Before I can respond, she continues, "I'm so sorry I haven't called—I've been tremendously busy with work and setting up the new house. It's beautiful! Cal is just going to love it. And there's a huge yard he'll have a blast playing in."

"It's okay—"

"And the weather, oh dear, it's just wonderful! The temperature is perfect — not too hot. My neighbors are great. They gave me the number of the gardener and invited me over for cocktails this evening. We had so much fun! Their kids are already in college, but they said Cal will just love the middle school here."

A timer beeped somewhere off in the distance, and I hear her say, "I have to go, but I'll call you later—I want to tell you more about the house."

I stand there, blinking, feeling like I've just been sucker-punched. Wondering—*is that how she always is?* After being with Zeke and Levi, who asked a million questions and seemed genuinely interested in us, talking to my mom for forty-five seconds has me second-guessing everything—again.

There are only three weeks until Cal finishes school. Eight weeks until he's supposed to move to Florida. That feels like no time at all to figure out what the heck I'm supposed to do.

Cal comes out of his bedroom, heading straight for the fridge. He was quiet most of the trip, playing a game on his phone, but there was this small moment when, out of nowhere, he said, "Pops was pretty cool. My dad was, too..."

"I think so too," I say softly. "He really wants you to be part of his life—if you're open to it."

He stopped responding after that, but the way he bobbed his head told me he was processing everything.

I didn't push after that, let him play his game while I tried my best not to think about what I just stepped in.

Do I regret bringing Cal to meet his dad? Not even a little. Does it scare the hell out of me? Absolutely.

Levi made me promise I'd keep in contact with him—he even asked Cal if he could text him. I could tell he was nervous, even asking, but Cal just smiled and said cool.

Slowly, I start unpacking, tossing the two days of dirty clothes on the floor while pulling out the nearly seventeen days' worth of clean outfits I packed, and carefully hanging them up.

I glance around my room and am reminded I do love it here. I turned my walk-in closet into a podcasting room and although I've definitely outgrown it, I don't mind it. It's moody and dark, opposite of the bright, colorful bedroom I have—kind of like me. Bright on the outside, moody on the inside—*or maybe, the opposite. Depends on the day, I guess.*

I've always liked this condo—liked raising Cal here, where we knew the neighbors, and they all invited us for Thanksgiving. Usually, only Cal and I went because my mom was working, but we still had fun.

I wonder what Thanksgiving looks like for the Turners. I'm sure they often have to work, too, but I get the feeling they do big family dinners when everyone can be together.

Should I ask him? He said I could text about anything, and I think this might be a good way to start that conversation between the three of us.

On impulse, I rip my phone from my back pocket and text Levi in the group chat he created before we left, titled "Canada or Bust🇨🇦"—him, Cal, and me.

Canada or Bust 🇨🇦:

> Thanksgiving dinner? The holidays in general —what's the Turner tradition?

I toss my phone onto the bed and get back to packing.

Ten minutes later, a voice message pops through, and I nearly melt when I hit play and hear the laughter in his voice.

"Figured it'd be easier to ramble over a voice message— Olivia's very into sending them lately. Anyway, most of the family has rotating shifts, so it's pretty damn hard for all of us to get holidays off at the same time—actually, almost impossible. Think it's only happened twice in the last ten years. So, we usually plan a family dinner on a different day. Used to be at Dan and Olivia's old house, but now that she built the new one, that's where we have it. I'm guessing it'll be the same this year, but I swear, each year it gets bigger and bigger. You'd both love it. Maybe we can figure out a way to get you here! Or not—no pressure, ya know. Uhm, yeah, so... The station guys always host a Thanksgiving or Christmas dinner for anyone on duty—fire or sheriff. Kind of an open-door policy, and everyone just stops by. It's fun—lots of teasing, but we all grew up knowing each other for so long, it's basically one big insult-throwing contest... What about the Dubrow family? Caviar shaped like a turkey?"

I can't help but laugh. The way he says it—without judgment or malice—feels so genuine.

Cal's head peeks through my doorway, smiling. "How does he know grandma likes caviar so much?"

"Lucky guess?"

"Or maybe Mom mentioned it back when they were together?" I try not to let my smile fade, but of course, Sienna could've said something. And yet, I feel a tiny pang of jealousy forming. *Nope—get it together, Aubrey.*

"I wouldn't be surprised. Grandma's been eating caviar bagels for brunch almost every Saturday as long as I can remember," I reply, forcing nonchalance. "There was this fancy restaurant in Bend she loved to go to with friends. Your mom and I hated it, though."

Cal crinkles his nose, feigning disgust. "I probably would've hated it too." Then he turns and over his shoulder yells, "You reply! I'm going to shower."

"Good, ya stink kid!" I shout teasingly and hear him laugh before the door closes.

I look back at my phone, nerves tightening in my chest. *God, I'm a mess.*

What do I say?

Okay, okay.

I hit record, start to speak, but nothing comes out. The little red lines start moving—my mind drawing a blank. I quickly hit stop and delete. *What's wrong with me?* I talk to myself every day—that's literally my job.

Sighing, I sit on the edge of my bed and try again. "That sounds fun! The Dubrow holidays are actually pretty low-key. Mom always works, so Cal and I usually have something delivered and pig out on the couch with movie marathons. One year, I attempted an entire Thanksgiving feast, but the only food that was edible came from a can or a bag."

I hit send and fall back onto the bed.

What the hell am I doing? Crushing on my dead sister's ex —no, her boyfriend? *It doesn't even matter.* It's so fucking messed up that I shouldn't even be entertaining these thoughts. Yet here I am—feeling guilty, confused, unable to shake the attraction I feel—and it's tearing me apart.

Chapter Thirteen

Aubrey

Canada or Bust 🇨🇦:

LEVI TURNER:

What's on the agenda today, fam? 🤚

CAL 🍕:

School, school, homework, studying for a test tom. 😣

LEVI:

What class? If it's anything other than Chemistry I'm happy to help.

CAL:

Health. 🍆 💧 💦

LEVI:

Sure. Know lots about health! It is my profession.

I't's still early morning when the texts begin rolling in between Cal and Levi, and I can't help but feel a rush of gratitude. Levi is honoring his commitment to reach out as much as he can, and while it may seem small, I'm glad we didn't leave yesterday and everything suddenly turned awkward. As I read through their chat, a personal message from Levi comes through, and I switch over.

Levi Turner:

Shit. Is that the like the birds and the bees stuff? ALREADY?

Aubrey, I'm not ready. He's just a baby ya know?

Yeah, they covered that last year. Let me tell you, it was AWKWARD. I don't think Cal looked me in the face for a week.

Thanks for taking one for the team.

After I finish making Cal's standard peanut butter toast and cereal for breakfast, I send off my own text in the group chat.

Canada or Bust🇨🇦:

Don't forget to add cleaning your room to that list.

Ooooh, better listen to Aunnie

I t takes nearly an hour to get Cal out the door and to school,
shuffling him along while he grumbles the entire way.
Once I'm back home, I head straight to my mom's closet. I need
to look in that box again—and hopefully uncover the secrets my
mom is hiding. Or at least, reread the ones I've already found.

I grab the box and bring it to the dining room table,
spreading everything out so I can take photos of each item. Levi
mentioned that Lincoln—the guy who emailed me—would
want whatever I could find.

I can't help but wonder if I should feel worse about basically handing over evidence to Levi—things he might be able to
use in a custody battle against my mom. But my gut tells me I'm
doing the right thing. Sienna wouldn't have wanted my mom to
lie. She wouldn't have wanted Cal to grow up without Levi. I
don't know how I know, I just do.

I start with the divorce records, opening my notes app and
scanning each document, creating folders for each file. I barely
glance through them, though—there's no doubt my mom took
my dad to the cleaners and got everything she wanted in the
divorce.

Next, I scan all of Sienna's medical records. It's all medical
jargon that's way over my head.

Then I feel a pull at my heart again when I see Cal's birth
certificate. Guilt flares up—at least implicit guilt.

Moving on, I open the last folder—the one I hadn't looked
at yet.

The letterhead is a large, scrawling "M&W," and for a
second, I think I just saw it earlier. I stare at the logo, noting

how distinctive it is—and then it hits me: she used them for her divorce, too.

Does that matter? Again, I just don't know.

I pick up the next document—a printout of an email about the retainer fee. The next is another email, as if my mom printed out each one for safekeeping. I scroll through the messages, feeling a mixture of anger and sadness, searching for anything that will give me answers.

But every page is vague—mainly just scheduling calls or meetings. They all start the day after Sienna was admitted to the hospital, and the last one is dated two weeks after we moved to Tacoma. It simply says:

Congratulations on your new baby boy, Rosa. Please contact me directly if you have any questions or concerns. I'll be in Seattle at the end of the month and would love to have dinner.

I'll call.

My best,

M. Mitchell

Was my mom...? Was she dating her lawyer?

I'm left with even more questions, my head spinning, wishing once again I could ask Sienna what to do.

Levi Turner:

The next is a photo of the console in a shopping cart while he waits at a check-out to pay and the amount of games he has next to it is nearly sickening.

Levi Turner:

Also super rusty, haven't held a controller in years. 🎮

Will I lose cool points if he kicks my ass? 😳

I can't help but laugh, the anxiety that was coursing through me evaporated at this goofy ass grown man.

Levi Turner:

Did you have cool points to lose? 😌

Not enough to bargain with. What makes old guys cool these days? 🤔

Are you an old guy now?

He's eleven! When I was that age any one old enough to buy alcohol was OLD.

True, you're ancient then. 😅

Okay, Miss Youth. Is it weird or not? Because I'm about to go home and spend the rest of the day brushing off my Halo skills and pretending I'm not over thirty.

Not weird, but work on your Minecraft skills first. He's still pretty in to it! I'll add you to his approved list of friends when you get it setup.

Thanks, Aubs.. 🙏 If it's a competition, I'll never catch up to your cool points.

Don't forget that I signed the waver to let him take the sex-ed class, pretty sure every cool point I ever had was wiped from the board and went into the negatives. 😬

Good point. Not in my book though—you got triple the points for that.

Chapter Fourteen

Levi

The music blares through the speakers as the crowd sings along and dances to Gwen Stefani. The energy in the arena is electric—there's a cowgirl behind me flying around barrels, her boots kicking up dust as she races around.

I glance up into the stands, recognizing the faces of the locals almost instinctively, but thankfully, there are plenty of people from out of town too.

I spot the crew near the top of the bleachers and make my way toward them. The EFSC guys sit at the very top, with Odessa and Maisie in front of them, and Everett and Isla a row beneath.

Greeting everyone, I settle next to Odessa and Maisie. I've known Maisie for over a decade—she's been like a sister to me—and Odessa, though she recently moved here, has been a good friend for years.

Maisie's knee-high boots and daisy dukes match Odessa and Isla's—*and every other other girls here*. I briefly wonder what Aubrey would wear to something like this—probably black denim shorts, black boots, the same edgy vibe she always has. I shake away the image of her quickly, though.

Leaning over to Odessa, so that Maisie can hear, I whisper, "Heard a rumor…"

"Don't you dare even go there, Levi Turner," she snaps in frustration, her eyes narrowing, and I can't help but chuckle. Maisie has been single since her high school love, Ethan, left for college—after a lot of bad stuff went down, she basically cut him out of her life. The rumor around town is that one of the EFSC guys, Leo, asked her out yesterday. Honestly, I'm surprised she didn't spiral into a panic—calling me a hundred times, analyzing every possible scenario. But instead, she seems calm, almost like she might be considering giving Leo a chance.

Odessa nudges me back to my spot, rolling her eyes, but even she seems to be giving Maisie the side-eye, wondering what's going on with her. I look back around at our group, noticing all the women around us have different shades of blonde, and again, my mind drifts back to Aubrey's fiery red hair.

"Beer?" Cooper, one of the EFSC guys—he's been sporting a mustache unironically for as long as I've known him—asks, snapping me back to reality. He's a good guy, and honestly, all of them are, but Coop's the easygoing one. Always chasing tail and up for a laugh—*much like what most people think about me.*

I shake my head, even though I really want to say yes. I'm not in the headspace for drinking tonight, and I wouldn't be surprised if I get called in somewhere along the way anyway.

Glancing down into the arena, I notice Luke is staring—more like glaring—up at me and Odessa. He's in his full

Cascadia County Sheriff uniform, sitting on his horse, Scotch. I can't help but grin even wider as his scowl deepens. Any time he channels his inner 'God of Thunder,' like he's about to turn into Thor, I just laugh. He may clearly be annoyed that I'm sitting next to his girl, but I know it's not about me. He's just being territorial now that he finally has her back.

"Luke and Odessa sittin' in a tree..." I start the teasing chant, and all the other guys join in as they start walking down the steps. "K.I.S.S.I.N.G."

"That's not all we're doing," Odessa shoots back with an evil grin.

Maisie protests loudly, "Eww, he's my cousin."

I look back over the crowd, and see the large brooding man who is the one and only Ethan Flacco walking up the stairs toward us. *Oooh, this just got interesting.*

If I didn't notice how Maisie tensed up, I might have a few more jokes in me, but I can tell she's really trying here. Usually, she avoids Ethan like the plague, but something has shifted—it's not quite Leo or maybe it is, I'm not sure.

"Hey," Ethan says, sitting next to me—taking up more space than the average person. He's a former NFL quarterback, never missed a meal or a workout.

Odessa leans over me to avoid shouting over the crowd. "Where's Jake?"

I glance over, wondering where his son is. Normally, he'd be here with Ellie and Ben—probably eating so much sugar that they'd be bouncing off the walls. But Olivia said she was too pregnant to be at the rodeo tonight, and honestly, I can't blame her. It's packed.

"Uhm, hello? What about me?" Ethan grumbles.

"You're a close second. But he's our fav."

They chat around me, but I focus back on the event. It's still barrel racing, and I can't help but think about Cal and

Aubrey—wishing they were here with me. I've already sent them a few photos, one of my arm wrapped around JJ Harris, the best rodeo clown out there, and a few of me working last night.

They've been gone for almost two weeks, and even though we talk every day, it feels like the longer they're away, the bigger the hole in my chest becomes. I just want to tell people about them—brag about how incredible my son is, how cool Aubrey is. I've been binge-listening to her podcasts, and holy shit, she's got a way with words.

Cal sent me some videos Aubrey took of him playing flag football, and I've watched them a dozen times. He's got a natural talent that I can't wait to tell Ethan about.

"Move, Turner." A deep grumbling voice has me looking up to see, my dear friend, Luke threatening from where he stands in our row.

"Excuse me," I demand, my hand going to my chest. "Is there a problem, Sheriff?" It takes all of my constraint to not grin at his pissed off face.

"Yeah, my girl, my seat," Luke nearly smiles, "Or your ass in handcuffs sitting in the back of my car."

"Oh, does he always talk this dirty?" I gasp, looking at Odessa, who laughs even harder.

"You have no idea..." she replies, a mischievous grin once again spreading across her face.

Everett, who's been in his own little bubble with Isla, looks up and immediately starts gagging at his sister's comment. He looks like he could pass for Odessa's twin—despite being a bit older—with his white-blonde hair and model features.

I stand up, giving a dramatic stretch before I finally give in and move back a row, trying not to laugh.

Then Luke makes an even bigger show, outdoing my

drama, by kissing Odessa in front of the whole town. *Guess that's the confirmation the town needed.*

And of course, because nothing in Three Sisters can go smoothly, I hear Ethan shouting, "What do you mean?!" into his phone.

Suddenly, everyone's on high alert, spines straightening as Ethan stands and continues yelling into the call.

Luke is right there, playing the role of the Sheriff—demanding answers. But when he says the next words, it's like my bones somehow know everything is about to change.

"Jake's missing."

The two of them storm down the steps, Maisie and Odessa close behind. I instinctively look to Everett and Isla.

Everett's face looks about how I feel—focused, in full problem-solving mode. His phone's already in his hand as he starts dialing—probably Drew or Hayes.

I turn to Isla, who's standing there, watching their retreat. She's completely pale—like all the blood has been drained from her face.

"Isla," I say softly, but she doesn't look up, only sways faintly, as if a gust of wind hit her. *She's not breathing.*

"Isla!" I shout, jumping down the two rows of seats until I'm in front of her.

She gasps loudly, as if I just appeared in her line of sight after being invisible. Everett nearly drops his phone as he looks back and forth between us.

"You good?" I ask, trying to assess as best I can, even though my focus is on getting to Luke and Ethan—doing everything I can to find Jake.

She nods quickly, swiping at her cheeks where a tear has fallen. "I'm good, I'm good," she whispers, voice trembling.

I glance at Everett, who gently places his hand on her shoulder and guides her back down to the bleachers.

"Drew?" I ask, gesturing toward the phone.

He responds with a sharp, "Yeah," then brings the phone back to his ear.

"Isla, keep breathing, okay? In and out," I plead, trying to watch her for any signs that she might pass out.

She looks up at me, her eyes a little clearer. "Go! You're more needed with Ethan than with me. I'm fine now—I think I just forgot to breathe."

Without hesitation, I take off down the stairs, searching for the two biggest guys in Three Sisters.

Luke has his phone out, reading whatever message just came in, and suddenly, it's like the entire rodeo crowd has gone silent in my mind. He looks even more like some mythical god as he starts barking orders at everyone around him. Deputies practically stumble over themselves, scrambling to follow his commands.

I ignore Luke for now. He's clearly in the process of setting up the amber alert—part of his duty—and my own professional instincts kick in as I step toward Ethan. He's kneeling in the dirt, staring at his phone as if it holds the answers to where Jake is. Visually assessing him quickly, I see he looks completely out of it—shaken, yet still breathing, albeit raggedly. Medically, he appears fine—*his mom could probably use some Ativan, though.*

Ethan's mom, Winnie, stands behind Ethan and is clutching onto her husband, Bruce. Her face is smudged with streaks of red lipstick, tears streaming down her cheeks as she sobs uncontrollably. Her body trembles with grief, her cries raw and animalistic—an utterly heartbreaking sound I've only heard in the worst moments.

I've known Ethan's family forever. I feel for her—I really do. But my focus sharpens on Ethan. My gut tells me he's the one I need to be most concerned about. He's been through too much already, and this—Jake missing—must be the worst nightmare come true for him.

"Luke," I call. He doesn't look up.

"Sheriff," I shout, and Luke, who's been pacing while on the phone, finally turns to me with angry eyes—though I know it's not at me.

"I'm taking him to the control room," I insist. "They'll help us look through security footage. It might not be much, but it'll give him something to do, keep him occupied."

Luke's gaze drops, his eyes flashing with frustration. But the anger fades, replaced by a quiet, lingering worry. "Go," he says, voice heavy but firm.

"Ethan," I continue, aiming for a calm but commanding tone.

He looks up at me, still on the ground, and gives a small, steady nod.

"Come on, buddy. Let's go find Jake."

He stands, following silently behind me, his eyes scanning the crowd—now with a renewed sense of purpose, as if this is the first step back from despair.

And no matter how dark everything feels, I hold onto that hope. Because sometimes, hope is all you can do.

Chapter Fifteen

Aubrey

I'm in the middle of tidying up after dinner, plates in my hands, the faint hum of the evening settling over the condo. It's been a good day—Cal had a game this morning and crushed it. Then we went out for lunch, and we've just been hanging around the condo all afternoon.

That is, until the group chat pings. I freeze, glancing at the screen. A smile suddenly blooms on my face—Levi had been sending goofy photos from the rodeo, and they've made me laugh every time.

But then I see the message, and my stomach drops through the floor.

Canada or Bust🇨🇦:

LEVI TURNER:

Hate to say this over text, but I can't call right now. Jake, my friend Ethan's son, has been kidnapped. Luke's handling it—amber alert's out. Just wanted to let you know before it hits the news. We'll find him.

Suddenly, the world tilts. My heart races, and a sickening, icy weight settles in my chest.

Cal bursts out of his room, eyes wide and unfocused, mouth hanging open as he stares at me. His face mirrors my own—shock, fear, that primal fear that makes my lungs feel tight. I see it in his expression, the way his body trembles not only with fear but with energy—the need to help.

I want to reach for him, to reassure him, but all I can do is stand there, frozen. My heart pounds so loud I hear it in my ears. That cold, screaming fear grips me—and this isn't just a random missing kid. This is Levi's best friends son, a child he considers to be like a nephew.

I feel helpless, useless—like the ground beneath my feet is crumbling.

"Aunnie, what do we do?" Cal's voice is trembling, desperate.

I start to speak, but I have no answers. We're five and a half hours away, with just this one text and barely any details. I don't know what to say or do.

"We should go! Help them look for him!" His voice bursts out, full of anxiety and urgency.

I take a deep breath, trying to steady my racing heart. "I wish we could—"

"But?!"

"But I don't want to make it harder for Levi," I say carefully. "He's got his own community there, tons of people already looking. I guarantee that entire town is shutting down right now, all hands on deck. If we go, it's about us—about what we're doing. I don't want to distract from Jake's search. We need to stay focused on knowing they're out there, fighting for him."

He stares at me in silence, his eyes heavy with emotion. Then he sharply turns and slams his door shut. Whether that's good or bad, I can't tell. I hate that he's pissed at me, but I can't bring myself to drive those five and a half hours tonight —to a town where we might not even be able to help effectively.

Canada or Bust 🇨🇦:

> Please call us if we can do ANYTHING to help.

> We will drive there first thing in the morning if you need us.

Four hours later, my phone dings while I'm in the shower. Without even thinking, I scramble out, suds still in my hair to see what Levi said.

LEVI TURNER:

> Just got word—Maisie found him!!! Jake is safe!

> OH MY GOD! THAT'S AMAZING!!

> How?! Who would take him?!

My phone goes silent—no text bubbles alerting that he's typing. After standing naked in my bathroom for nearly five minutes, I finally set my phone back down and return to the shower to finish washing my hair. Still, I sneak a peek through the glass shower door every thirty seconds to see if anything has come through.

An hour later, I'm curled up in bed, still waiting for a text. I don't expect one from him, but I'm desperate for more information. I've been stalking everything related to Three Sisters and their news sources for hours, hoping for crumbs, but it's mostly rumors and gossip still.

After a little longer, my eyes grow heavy with exhaustion. I'm about to send Levi a "I'm going to bed, glad they found Jake" text when I see the typing bubbles in our thread. I wish I could say my heart didn't do that stupid pitter-patter thing, but of course, it does.

LEVI TURNER:

> Hey, Aubs. Sorry I just got home. Went to the station for a bit, no one wanted to go home until he was back with Ethan.

> Is he okay?! Are you okay?

As soon as it says delivered, the screen on my phone changes with an incoming call: Levi Turner

I answer softly, voice barely above a whisper, "Hi," breathless from everything that's happened.

"Hey. What are you doing up still?"

"Couldn't sleep," I admit honestly, voice shaky but steady.

There's a pause, then Levi's voice drops into that comforting tone that always makes me feel a little less alone. "Yeah, I have a feeling I'll be the same tonight," he says softly. "This kind of stuff, it messes with your head."

"Is Jake okay? Ethan?" I ask, my voice cracking a little, desperate for reassurance.

He sighs heavily, and I can hear the exhaustion and worry

in his breath. "They're safe. They're okay—for now. Remember how I told you Ethan played pro ball but quit when he found out he was having Jake?"

"Yeah," I whisper, clutching the blanket tighter.

"Well," he continues, voice thickening, "that crazy bio mom convinced him to leave the rodeo—with her—despite Jake having no idea who she was."

My stomach twists painfully, and I feel the cold dread rising within me. "Oh my God," I breathe out, voice trembling.

"I know," Levi replies softly. "It's insane. Just... so messed up. And I don't even know how Maisie got involved. I only heard secondhand, and I haven't talked to them yet."

I take a deep breath, feeling oddly calmer just hearing his voice, even through the phone. The tension in my chest relaxes just a little, the tight grip softening.

"Are you okay?" I ask, my voice trembling with a mixture of worry and exhaustion.

He hesitates before responding, "I'm... No. There's been so much shit lately—scares, tragedies—nothing to do with the kids. But, this... who the hell does that?" There's a pause, then he adds, "Other than the fucking Puerto Rico guy."

I let out a shaky laugh, feeling the tension in my shoulders ease just a bit. Even after everything, he's so easy to talk to.

"Assholes and crazy people," I say softly.

"Is Cal okay? I probably shouldn't have sent that frantic text to both of you."

"He was ready to call in the cavalry—meaning us. He was actually mad at me when I said we couldn't drive there tonight."

"That's sweet," Levi says, yawning. "He's the best. Got a big heart, just like his aunt." My chest swells at his words.

I stay quiet, and after a moment, Levi adds, "Thank you. For bringing him to me. I don't think I said it, and even if I did, I can't say it enough. It's been the best month of my life—getting to know him. And you." *Is he... flirting? No.*

"Thanks for being the kind of man you are. You have no idea how glad I am you're not a loser deadbeat dad."

He chuckles softly. "Me too."

We sit in silence for a moment, my eyes feeling heavy as I listen to his steady breathing. The quiet stretches between us, comforting in its calm.

"Hey, Aubs. You still awake?" he whispers softly.

"Yeah," I whisper back, even though I'm barely holding on to consciousness.

He says nothing, but just as I begin to drift into sleep, I swear I hear him murmur, "I really hope I get to keep you both..."

Chapter Sixteen

Levi

I send off a text to the group, like I do every morning.

Canada or Bust 🇨🇦:

> Good morning, fam! Last night was intense. I'm sure Aunnie will fill you in on everything, C, but just wanted to let ya know that Jake is home safe, and Maisie is staying with them. I spoke to Drew this morning, and Hayes is heading out to Ethan's house today with Luke to get some answers. Stay safe, you two! Just got ya in my life, not ready to lose ya.

Over the last few weeks, I've definitely gotten more comfortable with my verbal affirmations. I don't want them to doubt, even for a second, that they're wanted—needed —in my life.

I'm taking an earlier shift, covering for Jed so he can get home early to his new baby. It works out—clocking the overtime now so I can take a solid two weeks off when Cal and Aubrey arrive.

The group chat starts rattling off—this one between the girls and me. I have no idea how it started, but somehow I was indoctrinated into their chat a few months ago. I usually stay quiet because I like to listen to the gossip, and I'm afraid if I say too much, they'll kick me out.

Spilling Tea 🍵 :

ISLA MITCHELL:

DOES ANYONE KNOW ANYTHING? I'm going crazy over here worrying.

2FG LIV 🧍 :

Andrew said Hayes is sending Linc and Liam to the house as extra security.

ISLA MITCHELL:

Did something else happen?!

ODESSA ASTOR :

Not that I've heard from Luke. Sounds like they're just doubling up for safety reasons!

3FG CHARLIE 👱 :

Hayes is on fire right now. He's pulling no stops. Bitch better run, because daddy Carrington is on a war path. 😨

ODESSA ASTOR:

Luke too! Kinda hot.

Also, annoying AS HELL. I'm on lockdown until further notice for "disregarding my own safety and well-being to go on a wild goose chase."

F uck. This town and its rumors—once they start, there's no stopping where they'll lead.

I gnoring whatever messages they're sending, I start to type in "Ca" to call Calvin. The name that pops up before his is Cal—my Cal. A rough, half-laugh escapes me as I make the connection once again. I'm not ready to tell Calvin that I've fulfilled my end of the deal yet, but damn, it hits a sentimental spot in me.

Calvin answers on the first ring. "Assuming you're calling about the Maisie ordeal?"

I let out a breath, rubbing my neck with my free hand. "Yeah. Think this town's had enough of the smear campaigns."

"Got that right. Elise and I are calling everyone, reminding them that silence is the best policy right now. Is the 'bod squad' able to watch out for Maisie and Jake while they try to catch that crazy broad?" I chuckle silently at hearing an old man use the nickname the town girls have given the EFSC guys, but I don't comment on it.

"Yep, sounds like Hayes and Luke are working together to make sure nothing else happens."

We say our goodbyes, and I settle into the quiet corner of the firehouse break room, a space that feels familiar and worn from years of use. I've spent nearly as much time in this building as I have in my own home. My home away from home—a place where I'm so comfortable I can be myself. The metal tables are scratched and scarred, and the fluorescent lights hum softly overhead, casting a dull glow over the cluttered counters. The faint scent of strong coffee and grease lingers in the air, but it's comforting. Despite the chaos that comes with our job, this room normally feels peaceful—calm before the next call, a brief lull in the ongoing rhythm of adrenaline and action. It's a steady, grounding energy, like everyone here knows exactly what could come next, but for now, we simply exist in this calm, collective space.

I check my phone, hoping for a response from Aubrey, but so far, only Cal has been replying. I don't necessarily mind—any chance I get to connect with him is a win—but something feels off. Normally, Aubrey would've responded a few times by now, chiming in with her own little quips or comments. I chalk it up to her being busy with work today, but there's still that small part of me that's wondering what's really going on.

Larry walks into the dining area with a confident grin, his shorter frame brimming with enough energy to break me out of my thoughts. He's been part of the crew for a few years now— still young but already comfortable in his own skin. He carries a large pot, steam curling into the air, and a handful of spice bottles in his other hand.

"Got something special for y'all," he announces, setting the pot down on the table. The aroma hits first—spicy peppers, garlic, and something savory. The dish looks decent enough—sticky, tangled pasta coated in a fiery red sauce.

"Paige made it and dropped off the leftovers," he adds. Paige is Larry's wife and also works as a dispatcher at the sheriff's office.

The guys gather around, eyeing the pot.

Hudson, my partner for the shift, raises an eyebrow, throwing Larry a skeptical look, his bushy grey eyebrows bunching together. "Whoa, Lar," he groans, already clutching his stomach. "That looks like I'll be needing Tums for the next week."

"Yeah," I add, giving Larry a teasing shove. "Careful, man—those old guys can't handle anything hotter than 'Crystal' anymore."

Larry just chuckles, totally unfazed. "Hey, my kids eat this no problem. You'll be fine!" I'm once again shocked he has kids—multiple, at that—especially at his age. He's not even twenty-five, and him and Paige already have three kids between two and five.

The guys toss around a few more teasing jabs—lighthearted firehouse banter—but honestly, I don't mind the heat. A little spice always beats bland, especially in the dispatch of a good meal. Plus, it's a good distraction from everything floating around inside my head.

The rest of the morning slips by in a blur—no calls, no emergencies. I've tidied up, helped with lunch, and messaged Cal and Aubrey a few times. Then the radio crackles to life.

"Medical emergency, apartments just off Main Street," the

dispatcher announces. It's an older, smaller complex we don't frequent often.

The truck pulls out ahead of us, Hudson climbing into the driver's seat, taking his sweet time with his check before finally rolling out in a slow, deliberate pace.

On autopilot, we make the quick two-minute drive. Even from a distance, I can see Liam, Cooper, and Leo standing over someone lying on the ground. My stomach tightens on instinct, eyes narrowing as I strain to confirm—then, as soon as I see her —Maisie—I'm throwing the door open and sprinting toward them.

I didn't notice Larry already there, checking her pulse— doing the standard procedure—but I'm pissed he beat us here. We leave the same station, but they got to her at least a minute before us. *There's no fucking excuse.*

"Back the fuck up!" I bark a little too harshly, my voice edged with a rare, sharp anger. *But this is Maisie.* I know how to handle this situation—it's happened too many times before.

Larry stands abruptly, hands raised in a defensive gesture, backing away. I drop to my knees beside her. My pulse drums in my ears as I assess her—her body limp, her face pale. The helplessness rises and tightens in my chest.

Her eyes flicker between consciousness and unconsciousness. Concern etches deep lines across her face as she lies perfectly still, and I feel that sinking, overwhelming feeling of powerlessness creeping in.

"Maisie, it's Levi. I'm here," I say firmly, confidently.

She's not even close to being out of it, but I catch her blinking twice at my voice, clinging to awareness.

"You're okay. It's not that night. You're safe now." My eyes scan her—watch her struggle to focus, to breathe. Her arm is wrapped around her waist, trembling as she holds on.

She hasn't had a panic attack this bad in years, but I

remember the first one like it was yesterday—how helpless I felt, sitting there on the floor of Maisie's, watching her look both terrified and utterly lost.

I don't need to check her pulse—I can see her heartbeat pounding in her neck, throbbing wild and thunderous.

She's so caught up in those memories that all I can do is repeat the same reassurance over and over, trying to break into her mind and bring her back to the present.

"Maisie, it's Levi. You're safe now, I'm here, and you're not alone," I say again, voice steady but gentle, anchoring her to reality.

Seconds stretch into eternity. Then, her eyes begin to focus, locking onto my face, and I breathe out a long, quiet relief.

"Breathe, Mais," I urge gently, my tone collected but insistent. "In and out. Just like we practiced." I see her try to match my rhythm, but each attempt is jagged, heavy. Her body fights my words and I can tell she's still battling shadows, shadows I've seen before.

I press my hands lightly to her cheeks, grounding her. "You're safe," I repeat, my voice steady. "Inhale... One, two, three, four. Hold... One, two, three, four. Exhale... One, two, three, four." Her eyes flicker to mine, clinging to my words. I can feel her concentration funneling into each breath.

She begins to focus, slow and deliberate. I can see her fighting the storm inside her, the wildness easing just a little, enough for clarity to peek through. I keep my gaze locked on hers, patient, unwavering, willing her to emerge from the darkness.

"Focus on what you can feel," I guide her, in the way I've done before, trying to shift her attention. "Focus on what you can smell."

Gradually, her breathing steadies, the ragged edges smoothing, each inhale and exhale softer. I see the tension loosening in her shoulders as she begins to recover. I stay close, my eyes never leaving hers, offering silent reassurance that she's not alone.

Her voice, shaky but steady, comes out, "I'm okay. I'm okay." She breathes heavily, exhaustion washing over her. I sit back on my heels, feeling proud she's fighting her way back, but I can't hide the relief in my expression and I have to blink away tears.

Luke's voice comes from behind me, and I instantly straighten up. "Shit, Maisie. A panic attack?" He asks gruffly, voice thick with concern. "You haven't had one in years."

She glances around at the guys, checking to see if they're paying attention and when she sees that they're all in conversation she looks back at me.

Gently, I ask, "Want me to check your vitals here, or in the back?"

Mumbling more than actually saying it, she gestures toward the spot right here.

It doesn't take long to check her vitals, and after a few minutes, I breathe a little easier, confirming she's going to be okay.

"Alright, you're slowly coming back to a normal range," I acknowledge. Then, quietly, so only she can hear, I lean in and add, "We are talking about this."

I glance up just in time to see Ethan barreling toward us with Jake over his shoulder. His face looks like he's ready to burn the world down, and a sickening sense of guilt hits me hard as I hear him yell, "Maisie!"

Ethan's always been a decent guy—damn good, a few years younger than me, and best friends with Olivia. I'd consider him a good friend, but until now, I hadn't even realized the secret I was holding for Maisie. A secret I'm not sure was worth keeping, especially when the truth is how much Ethan loves her. Life's too damn short.

"Are you okay?" Ethan's eyes scan her face like he's searching for the answers he doesn't have.

Maisie mumbles something in response, but my heart clenches when I see Jake climb into her lap, hugging her tightly.

"Uncle Luke called and said you fainted like one of those goats does!"

She laughs hard. "I did. But I'm okay now. Levi helped me work on my breathing—like we practiced—and I'm feeling better."

Jake looks up at me with wide, confused eyes. "You had to practice breathing before?"

I try to play it cool, but I can feel Ethan tense beside me.

"Yep, it's part of the job. I help people stay calm when they're feeling overwhelmed or anxious. It's important to know how to handle those situations," I explain.

"What can we do?" Ethan asks, glancing from Maisie to me.

"I'll leave that up to her. She knows how to handle panic attacks," I reply, planting my feet and stepping back. I turn away, heading over to talk to Hudson and the guys.

As soon as I make it over, I give them the rundown—she had a panic attack, which isn't uncommon for her, as she used to have them frequently. Considering it's a small town and everyone knows what happened last night, they don't ask any more questions. I overhear Cooper on the phone.

"Yeah, her apartment is completely fucked up, Hayes. I'm talking everything destroyed."

I walk over and give him a nod—like I'm asking without asking—and he puts it on speaker so I can hear Hayes, too.

"Fucking hell," Hayes grumbles. "Maisie's okay, though?"

That one I answer. "She's going to be. That was a bad one, but Ethan has her, and Jake seems to be calming her down."

"Fuck. Thanks, Vi. You good? I know you two are close..." I can hear the worry in his voice, and I know it's more than just concern about her—Hayes was there when Dan died. He's been a pillar for all of us, especially me. His calls always come when something traumatic hits, even if he isn't part of it. *He's good like that.*

"Yeah, man, I'm good. Just came over to see what you guys know. Did I hear right? The apartment was ransacked? Someone tore everything apart up there?"

Cooper nods, and I hear Hayes let out a long, steady sigh.

"We're handling it," he says simply.

If I hadn't seen the determination mingled with outrage in Cooper's eyes, I might've asked more questions. But there's no one I trust more than these guys. So instead of pushing, I simply say, "We don't take chances."

To which Hayes responds, "Never."

Once again, in this town, we can't fucking catch a break.

And on top of everything, I check my phone for the fiftieth time today, only to see there's not a single message from Aubrey. *What the fuck?*

Chapter Seventeen

Aubrey

Cal shovels popcorn into his mouth on the couch. It's late for a school night, but I honestly don't care. I feel off-kilter today, guilty. It all started when I woke up after dreaming about Sienna—nothing crazy, no accusations of stealing her life. Just that she was there, laughing in the kitchen while sitting at the counter watching Cal and me bake cookies. It felt so normal —talking, joking—until suddenly we were in Levi's kitchen, and it hit me: she was dead, she shouldn't be here. Then she was just gone.

I woke up with tears streaming down my face because she was so real, so vivid in that dream, and then—gone. I cried in the shower, thankful it was still early enough that Cal was sleeping. Because I'd gone to bed smiling, chatting on the phone with Levi, feeling important—only to wake up overwhelmed with the crushing guilt of what I'm doing to Sienna.

And if my emotions weren't already all over the place, Levi sent a very nice, very confusing message. I wish I could say I'm the type of girl who doesn't spend all day analyzing every sentence, but I'm not.

Stay safe, you two! Just got ya in my life, not ready to lose ya.

He means Cal, right? And me, by extension? After yesterday's traumatic event, maybe he's just being kind, including me. *Or...* maybe I'm not crazy. Maybe he actually cares about me, too. But in what way?

All day, I've been caught in an endless spiral of overthinking. Because, honestly, I don't want to admit it, but I have a crush—more than a crush, actually. *Dare I say... feelings?*

And how could I not? We text daily—he FaceTimes simply to check in or help Cal with homework—*and he's hot.* Every silly selfie he sends with some random person from his little town, the butterflies hit my heart hard.

But it's impossible to pursue anything.

So, I didn't respond to Levi this morning, letting Cal handle that one. He sent a thumbs-up photo—a quick shot of himself in front of the framed map we have in my mom's office. His thumb right under Canada.

Levi replied with a bunch of laughing, crying emojis—and then a picture of his waffles, covered in maple syrup.

I simply liked the original message, then slipped into my office closet for a few hours. When I finally emerged, Cal and Levi had exchanged dozens of texts back and forth. I didn't want to intrude on their debate about whether Canada's better than France—though, of course, I'd say France.

Out of nowhere, a piece of popcorn flies at me and I nearly jump out of my skin. I look up, and Cal's staring at me.

"Dad wants to know why you aren't responding," he says casually.

My jaw nearly drops—because one, Levi is calling me out and two why does Levi care if I'm not replying?

"Oh—uh, my phone's still plugged in," I deflect, gesturing toward my bedroom.

I give it another ten minutes before finally shutting the TV off. "Bedtime, dude."

He rolls his eyes but scoops up the popcorn bowl and puts it in the dishwasher.

"Brush your teeth!" I shout after him, and he grumbles, "Yeah, yeah."

I laugh softly, then head to my own room. Honestly, I haven't checked my phone in hours, but when I do, my eyes widen at the sight—ninety-five messages.

I shouldn't be surprised. We probably text that much every day, but today, it all feels... off.

Almost all are in the group chat, but there are three in a private thread with Levi. There's also a few work texts, most from Molly but one from the media company I work with. I don't normally respond on weekends, unless it's to Molly—so I save that one for tomorrow.

Instead I read through the private ones from Levi:

This morning he sent:

Levi Turner:

I know he's joking—trying to include me—but that pit in my stomach tightens.

The next one is a voice note and I nearly swoon listening to his voice. "Did you see that? Aubrey! He called me Dad! Holy shit, I'm—honored? I don't even know. I wasn't expecting him to cross that bridge yet, but damn— that has to be what it feels like when a baby says 'dada' for the first time. Maybe even better. Okay, I'm rambling. But, Aubs! Text us back! You're radio-silent today and missing out on the milestones!"

A different form of guilt hits, because I am bummed I missed that milestone. I've heard Cal say it a few times when he mentions Levi, but I can see how that would be a big deal for Levi.

The last text really gets me though.

Levi Turner:

Aubs, what's up? You okay? 👀

I fire off a quick text, trying to push down the strange guilt I've been stacking up. Levi hasn't done anything—this is all me.

Levi Turner:

Sorry I've been MIA! I spent the morning recording, then did a deep clean on the house since we're leaving next weekend. We sat down to watch a movie afterward, and I totally forgot my phone. I'll go through the messages now. Thanks for checking in!

I stare at the last message he sent, feeling the strangest mix of guilt and—dare I say—giddiness. *I'm a fucking mess.* One minute I'm berating myself for liking him, and the next, I'm preening for his attention.

Then I see the message change from unread to read, and

then my phone ringing with Levi Turner as the caller ID. *Damn, him and that way he always calls.*

For a brief second, I hesitate—*should I answer?*

Get it together, Aubrey!

"Hey," I answer, trying to sound casual, even as nerves flutter in my stomach.

"She's alive," Levi's voice is warm and familiar, but I sense the underlying unease.

"I'm—sorry, today was..."

"Was what?" he prompts, encouraging me to finish, but I'm at a loss for words.

"Just... weird," I finally say, the first thing that comes to mind.

"Weird?" he questions, and I can almost see the raised eyebrows in his expression.

"Yeah, just had an off day..."

Softly, he asks, "You wanna talk about it?"

I hesitate, but then I remember—if anyone's going to understand the situation, it's him.

"Do you ever dream about Dan?"

I hear him inhale, then let out a slow, steady breath. "Sometimes, yeah. Usually only when I'm stressed. Did you—" He trails off, like he's unsure if he really wants to ask.

He doesn't mention Sienna much anymore, and I've been wondering if it's too painful for him. Back when we toured Bend, he had no trouble living out memories—talking about her with a kind of reverence. But since then, her name seems to rarely come up.

"I did," I finally respond.

He stays quiet, and I can't tell if he's waiting for me to say more or trying to figure out what to say.

After a moment, he speaks softly, "They're so real, ya know? It's like your mind is playing this dirty trick on you, but at the same time, you can't help but feel grateful you got even a tiny piece of them back."

Tears well in my eyes, and I nod. "It was so real—she was so happy. And I just... I feel so guilty, like I'm living her life now, taking her place."

He clears his throat once, then admits, "I feel that, too—often. With Ben and El—especially when I take them somewhere special or witness one of their firsts, and Dan's not there. But I fucking know—" He pauses, takes a shaky breath. "I know Dan would've expected me to step up—be there, cheering them on, having those hard conversations, being present for moments he can't be in. I get that our situation is not the same—I don't have them full time, and Olivia's always been their primary. But from the dead-sibling side, I get where you're coming from. And I know Sienna would be proud of you."

When I don't respond, he prompts gently, "Aubs?"

"Yeah," I reply, wiping tears from my face. I wish I wasn't so full of doubt, but I am.

"Listen," he says softly, "there's no bringing them back. And if we let it, the guilt of being the ones still here will slowly kill us. It's not your fault Sienna died. It's not your fault you're raising Cal. Or that—" He stops, then quickly adds, "uh, that all this craziness is even happening. I get why your day was thrown off. But don't shut me out. We're in this together now—one big, crazy Canadian family..."

I let out a genuine, almost choking laugh at his joke, the kind that catches me off guard and feels good for a moment. Despite the heaviness I'm feeling, his humor is a balm—a reminder that I don't have to carry this all alone.

"Thanks, Vi."

"You're welcome, Aubs."

Chapter Eighteen

Levi

Canada or Bust🇨🇦:

> Good news! They found the retched woman that kidnapped Jake. She's been arrested!! 🚗

Aubs Dubrow🙌🏻:

> Hey, didn't want to scare Cal. The EFSC guys don't think she was working alone so they're keeping a close watch on her and Jake.

> Good! I still can't believe all of this is happening. Have you seen either of them?

Because of HIPAA, I never told Aubrey about the panic attack, but since the apartment being destroyed was all over local news, I knew I could say that.

I pull my new truck into a spot at the T-ball fields, parking almost a mile away because I'm running late. I was FaceTiming with Cal while he worked on his final project for English—it's finally his last week of school, and I'm practically bouncing off the walls with excitement for summer break. For them to just be here.

Walking and maybe a little jogging, I head toward the dugout to wish Ellie and Jake good luck before their game. It's only been a few days since Jake was taken, but it's good to see him smiling and laughing with his team.

Ellie spots me first. "Uncle Vi!" she yells, racing over.

"My number one girl!" I scoop her up, tickling her before setting her down again.

Jake runs over next. "Levi! Guess what?"

"What?"

Before he can answer, his dad comes storming toward me like one of those hurricanes Cal's worried about.

"Uh, hold that thought, buddy," I say, hoping my tone isn't too dismissive.

Jake glances toward where I'm looking and sees his dad closing in, then looks back at me.

"Did you cut him off or something? Looks like he has rage road," I almost laugh at his misuse of the term "road rage," but I play it off casual.

"Think I forgot to clean my room," I reply with a wink.

Ethan grinds out, "Turner," motioning for me to follow him out to the outfield.

146

I follow behind like a kid caught skipping class—feeling like I just got called to the principal's office.

He spins around, and I can tell by the look on his face that I'm about to get a big ole dose of his misplaced anger. His son was just kidnapped, the woman he's loved forever is hiding a secret from him—and I know what it is. I'm also the only one close to his size he can let it out on, so rather than get defensive, I brace myself for the verbal onslaught, knowing he needs to let it all out.

"What the fuck, man? We've been friends practically our whole lives. I was there every day after Dan died. And now I find out that Maisie's been having panic attacks—and YOU'RE the one helping her? Why the hell didn't you tell me?"

I take a deep breath, letting his words wash over me—his hurt, his betrayal. He's right. I was there for her every day, helping her work through what she endured. It's not fair to him that it was me, but the alternative is that it was no one, and that's not fair to Maisie.

"For years, right? She's been hurting for years, Levi. You could have told me anytime. And the worst part—what hurts *me* the most—is that I know you know what happened. You've been lying to me all this time. Why? To protect some stupid-ass secret that's ruined my life?"

I nod, swallowing everything he's said, taking it like a punch to the gut. I've known—one of the few people in this damn town to know—and I've carried that weight and responsibility for years. But up until recently, I truly believed it wasn't my place to tell him.

But after everything with Cal, after finding out the truth, I'm not so sure where I stand anymore.

"Don't be such a goddamn pussy, Levi," he goads, his voice rough. "Fucking say something."

"You're right," I finally reply, my voice low and strained.

"In trying to be a good friend to Maisie, I was a shitty friend to you."

He shakes his head, his expression more disgusted than angry.

"What. Happened. She won't tell me. I need to know—man to man. I need the truth."

I lock eyes with him, wishing I could convey just how badly I want to tell him. I can feel his pain—sense it, live it, carry it. But it can't be me. I have to at least give Maisie the chance.

"It can't be me who tells you. And I feel fucking awful for saying that. But it needs to come from her. If I take that power from her... I'd be no better than the asshole who did it in the first place."

That last sentence hits him hard. I see his head jerk back as if I'd struck him. We stare at each other for another long second, and I know I said too much—almost told him what happened. But my eyes plead silently for him to drop it, just for now.

Thankfully, he does.

Without another word, he storms off toward the dugout, leaving a suffocating silence behind. And I feel the weight of that guilt crushing me—like an elephant, sitting heavy on my chest. This isn't even my secret, and I've been carrying it for years. All because I thought I was doing the right thing—protecting Maisie. But was it? Was Ethan really better off not knowing? I honestly don't know.

I barely watch the game, my knee bouncing anxiously as I try to soothe the gnawing anxiety roiling inside me. Rosa and Aubrey, hiding secrets. Maisie and I, holding back what we know. A decade—more—of Rosa lying to me, and me lying to Ethan by omission. After all, a lie by silence is still a lie.

"Run, Ellie, run!" Olivia cheers beside me, oblivious to the storm raging inside.

We're outside, but it feels like the walls are closing in.

One secret.

Two secrets.

Aubrey did the right thing—she told me.

But should I tell Ethan?

Risk betraying Maisie?

Are they the same?

A loud horn blares, signaling the end of the game, and my head jerks up.

Shit.

Maisie needs to tell him.

I lean behind Olivia, my decision final.

"Hey, Maisie," I don't even ask, this isn't really up for debate, "Let's go for a drive."

Olivia tenses next to me, but thankfully she doesn't question it.

Maisie refuses to look at me, but she at least relents and agrees to go.

I say my goodbyes to the kids, avoiding looking Ethan in the eye, but still waiting by the fence for Maisie.

We walk in silence all the way out to my truck, but when she gets in, she puts on her customer service voice, "When'd ya get this?"

It takes all of me not to call her out, but I know she's just nervous.

With a sigh that feels like it's been building for years, I mumble out "two weeks or so ago." I don't mention it's because I found out I have a kid and want something more reliable, or that I finally am starting to feel hope for the future again. Instead, I stay quiet until she's buckled and then start to pull out.

She mentioned that Cooper and Delta would be following us, assumedly because Ethan is still paying for her to have private security until things calm down with his ex and the potential other person involved.

I drive to the place it all happened—the night that changed it all.

The night I almost killed a guy for trying to rape Maisie.

The memory is always there, front and center, but parking in the same spot I was before hits me harder this time.

The fear I felt when I saw her climb into that scumbag's truck. I practically dragged Sienna to my own, yelling at whatever idiot blocked us so we couldn't leave. I drove like a madman, desperately trying to find her, and deep down, I knew he would go the long way back to town.

Maisie and I weren't even that close of friends then, but I was friends with Ethan—that was all that mattered.

When I saw the headlights barely peeking down that side road, I saw red.

I was halfway out of my truck, barely managing to throw it into park before I took off running toward her screams.

He was so bloodthirsty he didn't even hear me coming, but I'll never forget the satisfaction of that first punch—the crunch of his nose beneath my fist. It fueled me, until everything was a fog of rage, adrenaline blinding me to anything else.

Then Sienna was there, in my face, screaming for me to stop.

"Her name was Sienna," I say softly, the memory fading but still raw. "We'd been hanging out for a little while. Met on campus—things moved pretty quickly, actually. But then—" my voice cracks when I think of finding her on her apartment floor, the hospital where Rosa screamed at me, and the obituary weeks later—carefully written to make it seem like she'd passed long before.

"She died."

"What?" Maisie gasps, shock evident in her voice. "How? When?"

"Pulmonary embolism, I guess," I reply, uncertainty creeping into my voice. Was that what killed her? Aubrey had mentioned she was in a coma, kept alive until Cal was further along. Did they pull the plug? Did Rosa give the order when Cal was old enough to survive? The thought makes me shiver, wishing it wasn't so painful to ask the hard questions. Part of me wants to know, but the other is terrified of the truth.

"Her family didn't tell me much," I continue, my voice heavy. "They weren't exactly thrilled about me hanging around her. It was, I don't know, about a month after that night."

"Levi—I'm so—"

"I know," I cut in, and she looks at me with the saddest eyes I've ever seen. "I didn't bring you out here to unpack my shit, but it's relevant. It's why I am the way I am. If she hadn't been there... I wouldn't have stopped." I pause, and honestly, I don't think I'd regret it.

"And if you hadn't been there, he wouldn't have... stopped," she says softly, her hand reaching out, gently touching mine as if to offer comfort.

"No, he wouldn't have," I agree grimly. That guy was terrible, through and through.

"Kept tabs on him after that," I admit for the first time. "Well, Dad did."

Again, she gasps. "Your dad knows?"

"Yeah, Maisie," I say, a little too harshly, but it's insane to think he wouldn't have found out eventually. He was the sheriff of a very small town and the only person that could potentially bail me out of jail. "I had to tell him. Scottie could barely walk after—had to push back his boot camp for four weeks because of what I did to him."

"I didn't—I didn't know that."

"Well, we never really talked about it, beyond those times when I'd find you curled up, having a panic attack." I can't even begin to count the times I would find Maisie having a panic attack somewhere, it almost became a sixth sense of mine, an intuition that she was spiraling and I needed to find her. "Thought those were gone, by the way?"

"They are—were, I guess. I was already losing it over my apartment being ransacked, and then Leo thought he was being helpful and put his arm around me."

I nod once. "After Margie picked you up that night, Sienna and I drove him to the hospital. Her mom worked there as a nurse, and in hindsight, I think that's the night she decided not to like me. Anyway, I called my dad and his parents. You were insisting no one knew what happened, but I couldn't just let it go without telling someone. Scottie was in pretty bad shape, and I needed help figuring out what to do next. My dad and his parents had it out for sure, but Scottie eventually admitted he crossed a line while helping a friend with a ride home, and that he could 'see why I'd think more was going on.'"

"Your dad let it go?" she asks, disbelief creeping into her voice, and I don't blame her. Dad was known around town for being no-nonsense and by the book—unless, of course, he knew —legally—the book couldn't be thrown hard enough. I have a feeling I inherited my taste for quiet justice from him, the kind that doesn't hold back.

"On the condition that he left town and never came back. His parents ended up moving back to Montana, too."

"I heard that, but it was just town gossip—he got a job back there," she says, voice cautious.

"I think they were worried you might eventually come forward. Doesn't look good for the new pastor in town's son to be accused of attempted rape."

She recoils at the bluntness, but still quietly asks, "Do you know where he ended up? I haven't heard anything about him since he left."

"Dead," I answer matter-of-factly, unable to hold back. "He was dishonorably discharged a few years after he enlisted. I don't know the full details, but reportedly, he ended up on a fishing boat in Alaska. Then he went overboard—or was thrown." Part of me wishes it was the latter—that he pissed off someone like me, and they made him suffer, even if only a fraction of what Maisie has endured. I hope he begged for mercy, and they laughed in his face.

Her neck turns slowly, eyes widening as it sinks in.

"He was a bad fucking dude. Piss off the wrong person out there, and they might not even bother looking for his body." I know I sound callous, but with everything I've seen, I simply do not give a fuck about guys like that. *Good riddance, burn in hell, you douchebag.*

We sit in silence, both lost in thought about how one night changed everything. *Would Rosa have hated me so much if I hadn't nearly killed someone? Was Sienna so stressed about it that it triggered her P.E.?*

"Levi—" she loudly cries, so loud I jump in my seat, nearly giving myself whiplash, only to see tears streaming down her face.

"What?"

"How long after she died did you start helping me?"

"Right after," I admit slowly. "I had just left the hospital and was driving home. I was mostly in a daze—and then I saw Leilani pulling away and you just... fell." It was like one second she was in the window and the next she had disappeared like a ghost. Again, I don't even think I put the truck in park before I was out the door.

"I had no idea. I should've—" she gasps, her breath hitching like she's about to have a full-blown panic attack, before finally whispering, "I'm so sorry I wasn't there for you, like you were there for me."

"You may not have known what happened," I reply, my voice thick with emotion, "but you helped me through it. All those articles I was sending you? They weren't just for you."

The ache in my chest sharpens as memories flood my mind—footage rolling like a tape. Maisie's face, terrified as I looked down at her with that piece of scum on top of her. Sienna lying on her apartment floor, as if she were sleeping. Charlie's face the day she arrived in Three Sisters, eyes hollow from fear. Feeling Dan's life slip away beneath my hands—the warm blood pooling beneath my knees, soaking into my pants. Olivia upside down in her SUV, that look in her eyes when she mistook me for Dan. A hundred other faces of patients I've helped over the years, flickering in between.

Maisie doesn't know about my own sleepless nights—those endless replays of every decision, every missed chance. The screams, the last breaths that echo in my head—how helpless I felt watching people fade despite everything I did.

"Okay..." she finally answers, snapping me out of it, but she doesn't realize that my spiral has left me furious.

"Do you know what I regret about all this?" I say, my voice sharp and unfiltered. "It's not losing Scottie or what happened with Sienna. It's letting you handle it your way and wasting all this time away from Ethan."

He didn't fucking deserve me lying to him. Maisie chose his fate—ignored him, pushed him out without even giving him the chance to show up. Maybe I'm projecting, but the anger brewing inside me is real.

"That wasn't for you to decide," she snaps, bitterness lacing her words.

"No, it wasn't," I explode. "But you should have told him!"

She matches my tone, voice loud with defiance. "He wouldn't be where he is today if I had!"

"You don't know that," I lash back, voice trembling with frustration. "You don't know how he would have handled it or how he'll handle it now. I feel like I've been lying to him for so long—and I can't keep doing that."

I pause, taking a deep steading breath. "You need to tell him the truth. He deserves to know—*all of it.*"

"He's going to look at me differently—like I should have known better."

"Maybe. Or maybe he'll finally understand why you kept it from him. Either way, he deserves the truth—and the chance to decide how he feels about it."

"Levi, I don't know if I can..."

"The only thing keeping you from letting it go, from truly moving forward, is this secret. It's got you bound up, forever tied to this place," I point toward the road where it all unfolded. "The world has moved on and forgotten about the injustice that happened here. Scottie is dead—not through any fault of his own—but you're still alive, carrying this burden?"

I meet her eyes, steady and unwavering. "Let it go, Maisie. Don't die with this secret still inside you. Not when you have someone who loves you right in front of you, begging to help you release it. That man has proved time and time again that he loves you. Let him."

She pauses, eyes locked on mine, and I can almost see the words resonating within her—her shoulders trembling as the weight of them begins to sink in, her confidence gradually rebuilding moment by moment. Then she turns, voice trembling but resolute:

"Take me to Ethan. Take me home."

And that's exactly what I do. I drive her back, dropping her off, feeling the weight of the day pressing down on me harder than ever. The last few days—weeks, really—have been brutal, exhausting in ways I can't fully explain.

I miss Cal.

I miss Aubrey.

They'll be here in less than a week, but it feels like eternity. Until then, I cling to my daily texts with Cal and my nightly conversations with Aubrey. That's been the one thing keeping me grounded—my little constants amid all the chaos.

It's been the best part of my day. Today's no different.

Once I get home, I make a choice that's utterly reckless—something impulsive, driven by too much emotion.

I pour a glass of whiskey.

Then another.

And another.

And then I call Aubrey.

Chapter Nineteen

Aubrey

My phone rings right on time at ten p.m., and like Pavlov's dog, my stomach flips with a rush of butterflies.

It's been three weeks of talking to Levi every night. A lot is in the group chat, but he calls me every evening—sometimes quick calls while he's on duty and with the crew, other nights hours-long conversations—five hours, the other night, until three in the morning. And I didn't want it to end. Which means I'm royally and utterly screwed with the "don't fall for your sister's baby daddy" rule.

I slide my phone off the nightstand and answer, trying to sound casual. "Hey."

"Hey," his melancholy tone hits me like a punch to the gut.

"What's up? You sound down," I ask plainly, no beating around the bush.

He blows out a heavy breath. "It's been a heavy day. Things got heated between Ethan and me at the T-ball game, and then Maisie and I had this huge—necessary—conversation about some stuff that happened a long time ago." My mind immediately starts spinning—stories about him and Maisie, who he swore was just a friend the other day. I've noticed the way he talks about her, though—almost protective, like he does with Olivia.

He continues, "Then I got home, and I wasn't in the best mood—didn't really want to eat. So I started drinking... which, in hindsight, was pretty stupid, ya know. Now I'm in an even shittier mood—kind of drunk—and should probably go to bed, but I've been looking forward to calling all day. And... I dunno, think I'm blowin' it."

"Oh," I draw out, trying to figure out what to say. He's definitely a little tipsy, but I can't blame him for wanting to let go for a bit.

"What happened at the game? I thought you were excited to go."

"I was. I love Ellie and Jake. They did great, by the way. Ellie was so damn cute runnin' around the bases. And Jake—he's definitely going to be a pro athlete, like his dad."

I can't help but smile when he talks about his family. He loves them so much, it fills my own chest too.

"Yeah? Football or baseball?"

"Dunno. Could be pickleball for all I care—he's going to kill it wherever he lands."

I laugh at the little hiccup in his voice.

"No—" he sighs heavily again, "The game was good. It was before—and after."

"Oh?" I prompt.

"Yeah." His tone draws out the word, as if he's not sure how much he wants to say.

"Do you want to talk about it?"

"I don't want to bring down your night with all this bullshit," he says, but I hear in his voice that he really wants to talk.

"Don't worry about that. I'm always here if you need to vent."

"I know—you're good like that. Like, you're honestly the best person, really."

I chuckle. "Thanks. So... what happened? You said Ethan and you got into it or something?"

"Or something..." he mutters, then explains, "Ethan's going through a lot right now. His son was just fucking kidnapped by his own crazy—I dunno—egg-donor, basically. And then Maisie —his Maisie—you know, the girl he's been pining over for so long, I can't even remember a time he wasn't."

"Yeah," I say softly, "you mentioned he loved her."

"More than love, Aubs. He's been— I don't know—border-line obsessed with her since we were teens. And right when they were at the height of their relationship, she bailed. Of course, I know why. But no one else did. I couldn't even tell anyone that I knew why." His voice speeds up, becoming a little more animated, and my mind races to keep up with everything he's saying.

He mentioned Ethan and Maisie had a falling out, that Ethan never gave up hope, but he's never gone into the details.

"So, her rescuing Jake? That's what changed everything, right?"

"You'd think. But nope. Maisie is one of the most stubborn women I know—and, I know a lot of stubborn women. Anyway, she refused to talk to Ethan about what went down back then. And then, Ethan found out I knew, thanks to Maisie's panic attack the other day."

"She had a panic attack?"

"Fuck, I'm not sure I'm supposed to say that. All that HIPAA bullshit, but she's also my friend. I've been helping her with these attacks since before I even got officially licensed."

"Uhm, okay? I won't say anything... I'm just trying to catch up," I say, feeling a little overwhelmed myself.

"No, I get it," he says. "It's not you. But yeah, she's been having them on and off. They stopped for a while, but I guess her apartment getting broken into set the one she had last night off again."

"Oh shit. That's what you were talking about last night?"

"Yeah. It was the worst one I've seen her have. She was completely locked up for about ten minutes. Not sure I've been that scared in a long time. Well, maybe not in a long time— these past three and a half years have been... or maybe it's been longer. Fuck—how long has Charlie been here? I swear, her rolling into town with a damn stalker really set things in motion around here." He rambles again, his voice tinged with frustration.

"Wait, stalker?"

"Another conversation for another time..."

"Okay," I let that go, then ask, "So, Maisie still won't tell Ethan? You said you had a big talk with her after the game, right?"

I hear another loud exhale from him, but he doesn't reply for a moment.

"Is she okay?"

"She's fine. I think so, anyway. I thought I was—like, finally, we aired it all out—and she said she's going to tell Ethan. But then I got home and started hitting the bottle. Maybe she's not," he finishes with a heavy sigh.

"What do you mean?"

He's quiet for a moment—probably longer than he intends —and I can hear his breathing, slow and deliberate. My instincts tell me to give him space, to wait until he's ready to talk.

"Do you know why your mom hates me? From before Sienna's P.E.?"

My eyes squeeze shut, and it's my turn to remain silent. *Of course I know what happened.* Well—I know both Sienna's version and my mother's. Levi assaulted some guy who was giving a friend of his a ride home. According to my mother, there was a misunderstanding, and things escalated quickly. But Sienna's account? She said it was 100 percent justified—because the guy had attacked her, or at least threatened to. It's all hazy now, over a decade later.

"I've heard two different versions of that night," I finally say, voice trembling. "But I don't know yours."

"There's probably some truth to both," Levi replies, voice raw. "Yeah, I beat the hell out of that guy. And I won't deny that I'd do it again in a second. Aubrey, he tried to rape her."

The way his voice breaks at the end makes my chest ache.

Suddenly, it's as if the connection hits my head so hard I see stars. I barely breathe out, "Maisie."

Because of course, it all makes sense now—his protectiveness of her, the way he talks about her. I thought it was just that they'd been friends for so long, that he saw her as a sister. And maybe that's true, but it's also the shared trauma—something deeper, something unspoken.

"You're one of a handful of people who know," he says, voice dark and quiet. "Maybe a few more now. I dropped her off a few hours ago, and she was going to tell Ethan."

He mentioned it earlier, but I don't say anything. He's clearly processing everything, trying to get through the drunk fog of emotion.

"And that's why she's avoided Ethan for years," I trail off, feeling the weight of it.

"I kept that secret for so long," he finally says, voice thick with regret. "I don't think I realized how much it was eating away at me until you showed up. And now... I'm the one prolonging Ethan's heartbreak."

"It was Maisie's secret... not yours," I remind him softly.

"Ethan deserved to know," he says sharply, but I can tell that's not what he truly wants to say. What he wants to say is, 'I deserved to know'.

I remain silent. What can I say? He did deserve to know.

"Twelve years, Aubrey. Twelve fucking years," he whispers so bitterly it cuts deep.

"Wasted," he continues, voice low and crushed. "All that time—just... wasted."

I finally manage to whisper, my voice barely more than a breath. "I'm sorry," I say softly, my words lost amidst the silence. His absence on the other end speaks volumes—there's nothing more I can say to fix this.

"Me too, Aubs. Me too," he finally replies, hurt and resignation thick in his voice.

All I want is to reach through the phone and hold him, to comfort him, but I can't. I was part of the reason he's hurting, even if I didn't know it.

That heavy silence drags on, and I wish I knew what to say —how to make this right, how to go back and fix the wrong. To return to the normal conversations we used to have, but I don't get the chance.

Because I hear a quiet, "I should go to bed," and I can't do anything but respond softly, "Goodnight," before I hang up.

I sit there in the dark, holding onto the silence long after the call ends. I know he was drunk, I know he was projecting—yet it still cuts deep, a sharp reminder of my own guilt weighing heavily on me.

Chapter Twenty

Levi

My head pounds as I wake up, feeling like I've been hit by a truck—hard. The room spins slightly, and I know I'm paying for last night's stupidity. I stumble to the window, trying to make sense of the haze.

And then I see it—a broken glass on the floor, blood smeared across the tiles. *Oh, shit.*

The memory hits me like a freight train. I'd dropped my empty whiskey glass while stumbling to bed. I've never been one to get blackout drunk—at least, not like this. But the last month has been a constant explosion of turmoil: finding out about Sienna and Cal, Maisie's attack, Ethan blaming me for not knowing, everything bubbling up to the surface. *Why the hell wouldn't it all finally blow?*

I hurriedly hop on one foot to the bathroom, get my foot cleaned up, and slap a Band-Aid on the cut. It's a pain in the ass walking on it, but I dose myself with the highest dose of Acetaminophen I've ever taken.

While the coffee brews, I swallow the meds and sit at the

dining room table, trying to ignore the mess of broken glass still waiting. I rest my forehead on the table, feeling that familiar wave of regret.

What else did I do last night?

I jump up, hobbling into my bedroom to grab my phone. I have to be careful with each step—no more reckless mistakes. Then, a vague memory surfaces—the call I made to Aubrey yesterday, that frantic unloading.

A gut feeling telling me I need to call her again.

I dial and she answers on the first ring, her voice still sounding sleepy.

"Hi."

"What's your favorite flower?"

She pauses, confused. "Uh—what?"

"So I can send you apology flowers, or maybe chocolate? Drew pretty much bought all the peonies in Three Sisters, and I haven't seen a single white rose in the county, but I'll figure it out if that's what you like."

"Levi... what?"

"I was drunk and called you last night."

She hesitates a beat. "So?"

"So, I shouldn't have unloaded on you. I was way too caught up in my feelings about everything that's been going on, and I don't want you to think you're responsible for any of it."

"Oh..." she says softly, understanding the weight of it.

"Aubrey, I am so sorry."

"Levi, stop," she replies, her tone firm but gentle. "You have every right to feel how you do. It'd be more of a red flag if it didn't affect you at all. Especially considering the timing— Maisie's attack was around the same time Sienna died, then twelve years later, Maisie and Ethan go through something else traumatic with Jake. The timing—the timing is just... wild."

"It really is," I admit.

"But I'm not mad at you for feeling that way," she reassures me.

"I know, I know," I say quickly, "but I took it out on you."

"Not really," she responds. "Alcohol just heightens everything. You know that saying 'drunk words are sober thoughts?' I think that's bullshit. Drunk words are just the worst, most dramatic versions of your sober thoughts. The alcohol doesn't cause emotions—it just amplifies them."

"Yeah," I agree, albeit still hesitantly.

"You know what my dad used to say? 'Never drink to feel better—only to feel even better.' If you're in a bad headspace, it's only going to make it worse."

I nod, feeling the truth in her words. She's been talking about her dad more lately—little stories here and there—and I've learned that if I push too hard, she shuts down.

She laughs softly. "You were a little all over the place. How are you feeling this morning?"

"Like I got hit by a truck, but a little better now."

"Aww, poor baby," she giggles again, and I wish I could record the sound—to keep playing it. *I like her.* Out of nowhere, that thought hits me—unexpected, quiet, but sharp.

I quickly shake it off and change the subject. "You starting to get packed?"

It's only a couple of days until they get here. Cal has a half-day on Friday, and they're leaving right after he gets out of school. It works out perfectly, since I start my last shift then, and I'll be cleared to take three weeks off.

"Yeah, a little," she says. "I figured I'd finish everything on Thursday. I still have a lot of work to catch up on, but I'm hoping to record at least four episodes so I'm set up and can take a little break, too."

"That's awesome! How's Cal doing?"

"Better than I've seen him in a long time, actually. He already packed his bag—left out a few things for the last week—but he's beyond excited."

My chest lightens, and my smile widens. "Me too."

Chapter Twenty-One

Levi

"Finally!" I yell, jumping off the porch and heading toward Aubrey's car. Cal's already out, grinning from ear to ear, but Aubrey's still sitting inside, staring at her phone. Not exactly the warm welcome I was hoping for, but it's been a long drive, so I figure she's just catching up on texts.

"Bro, right? Aunnie drives like a grandma," Cal jokes as he walks over to me.

I chuckle and shrug. "Better safe than sorry. She's got precious cargo she's responsible for."

Finally, Aubrey gets out of the car, gives me a quick hug, and offers an apology. "Sorry, I had to check in with my mom," she explains.

My face must reveal my shock because she quickly adds, "She just thinks we're on a little road trip around the PNW..." and in a softer tone, she mumbles, "and even that was a stretch to get her to agree."

I nod, but I keep my silence. I don't really know where her head's at lately. We've only just touched on the folders she found, and most of our conversations have been light—mostly getting to know each other. No mention of custody battles or anything serious.

Cal grimaces and adds, "Yeah, Grandma tried to threaten to fly me out early, but Aunnie said no."

That catches my attention, and I blurt out, "You just said no?"

She shoulders up and scrunches her face as if to say, "I guess so." And for some reason, that simple act hits me hard—so hard I can't help but smile.

"Good for you, Aubs." Then, because I can't stand looking at her without feeling something stirring inside me, I turn my focus to Cal.

"Considering you're here, I'm assuming Grandma's threat didn't work."

Cal nods, a smirk playing on his lips. "Yeah, she's not happy about it, but oh well."

Aubrey shrinks back a little, and I catch her glance out of the corner of my eye—worry flickering behind her expression. I know she's still not entirely comfortable with all this, but I appreciate her sticking her neck out for me.

"Should we grab the bags and head inside? I made dinner, but it'll keep, if you already ate."

Shaking his head, Cal says, "Nah, not since lunch. And I'm staaar-ving." He heads toward the truck to grab a bag, and I follow.

I shoot Aubrey a worried look, hoping she'll meet my gaze, but she doesn't. Clearly, there's more she's not saying, and it immediately puts me on edge.

What the hell did Rosa Dubrow do now?

Knowing how Rosa is hurting her fuels my protectiveness even more. Without overthinking it, I fire off a quick text to Hayes, asking if he's got time for a meeting Monday morning. Almost instantly, he replies—he's free at nine.

The relief hits me like a wave. While I can see that Aubrey's still bothered, having a plan in place is enough to help me focus. I shift my attention to Cal and just try to be present for him, for this moment.

It isn't until hours later that Cal finally goes to bed. Honestly, the night flew by. We had dinner, played some board games, and laughed until we hurt. Aubrey's mood did a complete 180; she seemed to be genuinely enjoying herself.

I was finishing up the dishes in the kitchen when I caught sight of her walking back down the hall. Like those first nights they stayed—weeks ago—I had to remind myself a dozen times not to stare. She's beautiful always, but something about seeing her so at ease in my house makes her even more captivating.

Instead of sitting at the dining room table, she heads into the living room. I contemplate forgetting about the dishes and following her. But something in me whispers to wait—give her a few minutes to settle in before my presence bombards her with the unspoken questions from earlier—*or spoken if she doesn't offer them as soon as I walk in.*

When I finish the dishes, I find her curled up on the couch, wrapped in one of the blankets Olivia insisted I get—just in case I "ever have a woman over for more than an hour." *Didn't realize at the time how much I'd love that damn blanket, or having a woman on my couch using it.*

"Soooo," she softly drawls, the word stretching as I settle onto the couch next to her. *Sure—I could've gone to the other one, but this way, I get a better view of the TV.*

"She moved up the timeline. Wants him in Florida next week."

"What," I gasp, my eyes scanning her face for any sign of a joke, but I find none.

"I think she knows—feels the walls closing in on her or something—I swear, it's like a sixth sense."

"What do you mean?"

"After that first trip, she started calling more. Asking Cal and me about our weekend, what we were doing... Then this morning, not even ten minutes after I started packing the bags in the car, she called again."

"That the conversation Cal overheard?" I reach out, wrapping my arm around her, pulling her close. *Sure—I could play this off as friendly.*

"Yep. I wasn't about to tell her we were coming here," she reassured me. "So I said we were going on a little road trip. She went off on me—accusing me of hiding things, planning some trip I wouldn't be able to afford if I didn't live in her house. That was the real kicker. Because, yeah, it's her house. But the truth is, the only reason she can afford that place is because of the big settlement she got from my dad. I know she's a hard worker— that's why she took the new job! Ugh, I'm rambling, I know."

"You're not. Keep going. Get it all off your chest."

"It's just—Levi, I'm not some lazy freeloader living off my parents' dime. You wouldn't believe how much I made last year —I signed with a big media company, hired Molly, and I've got producers now. I'm not completely worthless."

The part that really gets me—the fact that anyone could make her feel this small—is beyond me. Especially considering everything she's sacrificed to help raise my son.

"Aubrey," I say softly, "if anyone makes you feel less than, that's a reflection of them, not you. You gave up high school, your teenage years, to raise your sister's baby. That's incredible —more than incredible. The sacrifices you've made are unimaginable. And then, you built this amazing career for yourself. You're far from worthless—you're perfect."

Her lower lip trembles just a little, and I wish I could kiss her, hold her close. Instead, I pull her in tighter, resting my chin on the top of her head. I hold her close, feeling her warmth and strength.

"You are the strongest person I know, Aubs. And I'm so grateful to have you in my life," I whisper.

She pulls away slightly, looking up at me, her long eyelashes framing her deep brown eyes. Her lips pout ever so slightly, and I find it impossible not to glance at them—*damn, if I don't move, I'll—*

Before I can finish that thought, she's leaning in and kissing me. I'm completely lost in the moment—feeling like everything is finally falling into place. One kiss, erasing every doubt and fear I had about us.

That is, until she pulls back, her eyes wide with surprise. "Oh shit."

I can't help but smile—part relief, part awe. I'd thought I was crazy for feeling this connection, especially with everything with Sienna. But maybe, just maybe, it's real.

"Stop looking at me like that," she insists, though I see her fighting her own smile.

"Come on, Aubrey," I tease, trying to keep it light. "*You* kissed *me*, after all."

She sighs. "I know. You said all those nice things, and my head's all over the place."

Laughing, I reply, "You and I both. But so what?"

"So what? Levi! We can't."

"Says who?" I raise an eyebrow.

"I don't know—society? Don't you think it'd be weird?"

"Oh no! What would the town say?" I joke, covering my chest with my hand, as if trying to shield myself from judgment. Then I soften. "It doesn't matter. I like you. You like me. Sienna and I? That was a lifetime ago, and it was special. But there's no..." I pause, trying to find the right words without sounding morbid, which is a talent I've developed over the years.

"There's no bringing her back," she finishes quietly for me.

"No—but, I agree, maybe your first day back is a little too soon for make outs on the couch," I tease with a grin, once again, trying to lighten the mood.

She smacks my chest, then lets her head relax on my shoulder.

"I don't want to mess this up," she says softly. "Cal deserves to have a real relationship with you. I want to make sure we do this right."

I nod, grateful for her honesty and her commitment to him.

"Either way, I promise it won't affect Cal," I pressed. "But I'm telling you now— I like you. I could see a future with you and Cal." Those words—so long unsaid—feel strange but right. It's been a while since I've even allowed myself to think like that, probably since Sienna.

She stays quiet, but I can feel her processing everything I've just said. Her tension eases as she leans into me.

"It's weird... how connected I feel to you," she admits. "I don't know if it's from all the phone calls and texts, or because I see so much of you in Cal, or maybe that whole Sienna connection. But it's soul-level."

"You been talking to Odessa without me knowing?" I ask, teasing, as I gently tickle her side.

"Oh yeah," she laughs. "Been chatting with your super-famous friend I've never even met— all the time." She has no idea that she's about to become best friends with my 'super-famous friend,' because once I tell them all about Cal, Aubrey will be included too. My people love hard.

"I take it she's into all the spiritual stuff, too?"

"The Astors are very 'woo-woo,' if you know what I mean."

"'Woo-woo,' huh? What does that even mean?" she asks, cracking up.

"You'll see. They're both into following your intuition—more in tune with things unseen. Everett's got a weird sixth sense about things, almost like a human pendulum, always in tune with the universe."

"Sounds interesting," she says, her curiosity piqued.

"And Odessa? She's like a human lie detector, but based on people's energy levels. She can spot a red flag a mile away."

She grins. "Great... now I'm not sure how excited I was five minutes ago to meet everyone."

I laugh. "They'll love you and Cal. I know it."

"How do you know?" she asks, skeptical.

"Because you're part of me," I say, my voice steady. Then, unable to resist, I add with a wink, "Soul-level, baby."

Chapter Twenty-Two

Levi

Another perfect day with my family.

That's all I could think about as we drove back from Redmond. I took Aubrey and Cal to Smith Rock for a hike, had a picnic lunch, and afterward, grabbed burgers on the way home.

By the time we pull into my driveway, it's late, and I can see everyone is tired—but I still want to spend time with them.

"Movie night? I'm feeling a little left out—I missed so much while you were back home," I suggest.

Cal laughs. "Oh yeah, definitely missed out on Aunnie falling asleep with popcorn in her mouth."

She turns around, mouth dropping open at his revelation. "Cal Sullivan Dubrow! You promised you'd keep that a secret."

"Oh, right..." he shrugs, then adds, "And I definitely don't have pictures!"

He quickly jumps out of the truck, running toward the house as she scrambles to follow. He's through the door, shutting it behind him, while she sprints up the steps. I'm right behind her, but before she goes in, I grab her hand and pull her back to me.

"Aww, Aubs! There's nothing you could do that I wouldn't think is beautiful."

Her eyes soften slightly, locking onto mine.

"Plus, I just met him! You can't go killing him now," I tease. "And I'm a mandated reporter, so I can't even be your alibi."

She roughly pulls her hand out, playfully shoving at my chest.

"You two are trouble!" she scowls at me, but I grab her hands again, pulling them between us.

Slowly, I move forward until her back is pressed against the door. Just as I lean in to kiss her again, my phone begins ringing in my pocket killing the moment. *Or maybe preventing me from doing yet another impulsive thing.*

Groaning, I pull it out, still keeping her pinned against the door beneath me. She's breathless now, her eyes shining with a mix of humor and lust.

"Luke," I answer, voice goading, "what could you possibly need at a time like this?"

"Maisie was just held at gunpoint," he responds sharply, and everything in my mind crashes—my heart pounds, my palms sweat, and a fog of panic envelops me.

Instinctively, I step back, my skin suddenly cold and prickling, eyes wide with alarm. I see Aubrey's mouth form a perfect "O," her face draining of color.

"What the hell happened?" I bark, harsher than I intend. "Is she okay?"

"She's safe—everyone's headed to Liv's right now. C.J. was after something in Ethan's safe and held Maisie at gunpoint, hoping she knew the code. Cooper was able to disarm C.J. with a clean headshot. Then Drew and Everett discovered Jason's involvement."

C.J.—Ethan—Maisie—Cooper—Drew and Everett—Jason.

"Jason?" I blurt out, equally demanding and questioning, as I try to piece together the names he threw at me. "Her brother-in-law?!"

"Yep," he confirms, enunciating the 'p' as if it offends him. "He figured out Stephanie and C.J. were in cahoots and wanted a payday."

"You're fucking kidding me." Stephanie is Jake's biological mom, the one who kidnapped him, and CJ works at Ponderosa Pine for Ethan. Jason's her sister Margie's husband—a sister she's very close to, her ride-or-die. *How the hell are the three of them working together? And why?*

"No, I wish I was," he replies grimly. "This stays between us, yeah? I shouldn't be calling you, but I know how close you are to Maisie."

I take a shaky breath, adrenaline still flooding my veins. "I appreciate it," I say quickly, hanging up, but my mind's already racing.

Fucking Jason. I've hated that guy for years. Marguerite—Maisie's sister—is a little older than me, as was he. We ran in similar circles back in high school; he had a legendary ego then, along with an even bigger drinking problem that only seemed to get worse with age. The number of times we've been called because he passed out drunk somewhere is about five too many.

"You should go check—," Aubrey begins to suggest, but I cut her off before she finishes her sentence.

"Yeah, let's go," I bark, my voice sharp.

I push open the door behind her, shouting, "Cal!" as I walk in.

"Cal! We gotta go," I say frantically, searching for my truck keys.

"Where?" he asks, walking down the hall, glancing

between us. I ignore him and keep searching, flipping over everything I can get my hands on.

"His friend Maisie—someone tried to hurt her," Aubrey explains quietly to Cal.

She reaches out, placing her hand on my arm, her voice pleading. "Levi, maybe we should stay."

"Nope," I say, patting my pockets—and then I feel it. I pull out the keys, holding them up like a trophy. "Found them!"

Cal walks out with a shrug, but Aubrey stays rooted as if she's digging in her heels. Instead of listening to her doubts, I simply scoop her up and carry her out the door.

"We gotta go, Aubs. No dilly-dallying."

She begins to protest again as I open the truck door for her. "But—"

"Buckle up," I interrupt, shutting the door and rushing around to the driver side.

It's dark outside by the time we arrive at Olivia's, but the driveway is packed with cars.

I shoot a quick glance at Aubrey before I open her door. I can tell she's putting on a brave face—almost wooden—doing her best to stay neutral. Even Cal looks a little nervous. And if it weren't for the extreme circumstances, I'd have waited to introduce them.

Even so, I hesitate before dragging them out of the truck. "Are you two okay with this?"

They both nod, and I try to offer a calming smile. "They're going to love you."

The front door opens into the formal living room—elegant furniture, a (mostly) polished atmosphere—nothing like the chaos to the right. To the side, an expansive open-concept kitchen and living room flow seamlessly into each other. From the entryway, I see everyone gathering in the kitchen, chatter and laughter filling the space.

Before I can close the door, a gust of wind slams it shut, making me spin around quickly, stepping around Cal and Aubrey. When I look up, I throw my hands in the air in mock-surrender—every man in the room is on their feet, hands resting near their concealed guns, eyes alert and tense.

"Sorry. The wind caught it," I call out, voice casual but aware of the tension in the air.

Thankfully, Maisie is closest—standing near Ethan. I nearly stumble over my own feet rushing toward her, pulling her into a hug.

"You good?" I whisper, squeezing a little tighter.

She nods against my shoulder, and finally, I feel a tiny sense of relief—like maybe the worst part is over, or at least I hope it is.

I step back, standing next to Aubrey and Cal who are practically radiating nervous energy.

When I look up, the entire group is still staring in shock, mouths agape.

"Holy shit, you have a kid!" Maisie's jaw drops, her eyes bulging wide.

Behind her, Cooper lets out a louder gasp, and everyone's neck snaps toward him.

"Did you hear that?!" he exclaims. "Maisie just said a bad word!" Then he claps loudly, breaking the tension with his usual goofy energy.

I clear my throat, then drape an arm around Cal's shoulder, grinning wide. "Everyone—meet my son, Cal. And this is Aubrey—his aunt."

Lincoln tilts his head, then a broad grin spreads across his face. I nod, confirming what he's thinking.

Then he exchanges a quick glance with Drew, and I briefly wonder how much everyone on the team knows. The girls rush toward us, though—my attention quickly shifting to them.

Olivia gasps, mouthing, "Cal," and I nod in response.

She's the first to reach us, rushing over with a bright smile. "Hi! I'm your other aunt—Olivia. And your cousins, Ben and Ellie, are somewhere around here playing. And this is"—she gestures to Drew, who steps forward next to her—"Uh —Drew?"

My face must give me away because she simply throws her hands in the air. "I mean, I don't know. Drew, Andrew, someday Uncle Drew? You'll find out soon enough—it's all one big, complicated family around here."

Cal's smile seems genuine, and he laughs. "Dad's talked a lot about all of you."

Olivia's eyes flick to me, as if the impact of him saying "dad" hits her too, and I feel my smile grow broader.

Ethan grins, too, looking at me and nodding his approval, then lightly shoves Maisie forward—more quickly recovered from the shock than she had been. "Ethan Flacco, and Maisie— some-day Flacco," he introduces. I chuckle softly as Cal's jaw drops; he knows exactly who Ethan is, but meeting him in person must still feel a little surreal for him.

Next comes Charlie, holding baby August, who steps into the group with a friendly grin. "Charlie, and August. Hayes, my husband and baby daddy, is around here somewhere too."

Aubrey and Cal nod politely, taking in the core group for the first time.

For a moment, an awkward silence settles over us, every-one's eyes flickering as they take in the situation. The energy shifts from excitement to questioning so quickly that I begin to second-guess my decision to bring them here.

What the hell do I say now?

Chapter Twenty-Three

Aubrey

The room went quiet fast—really freaking quiet—and Cal and I exchange a quick glance before I finally decided to take one for the team.

"Hi," I say, trying to sound casual, my voice a little unsteady. "Like Cal mentioned, we've heard so much about you all. I'm sure we're just one more surprise to your 'holy shit' of a day..."

They all laugh, and one of the guys, Cooper—who hasn't been officially introduced—chimes in, "Could say that again." He's just as attractive as every other guy in this room, and I feel myself starting to blush as everyone laughs.

Soldiering on, I continue "We don't mean to intrude. Levi just kinda threw us in the car, mumbling about all the crazy-ass people in Three Sisters these days and not wanting to leave us alone. Obviously, he explained on the way—" I trail off, nervous again with all eyes on me. "But, yeah, sorry to drop this little bomb on you," I finish.

"Are you kidding?" Olivia wraps her arm around me, still smiling. "Any time is a good time to find out about new family

—trust me, with this group, news is never delivered delicately at the right moment."

Suddenly, Hayes appears behind us, stepping around Levi — *Again, another hottie. Tall, dark hair, chiseled jaw. Pictures do not do these men justice*—and says, "Yeah, pretty sure I told Liv about her own estranged bio-dad when she was in the hospital recovering from a roll-over MVA."

Olivia's eyes widen excitedly, and she smiles brightly. "You did! And now I talk to him every day."

Drew huffs before walking back toward the kitchen, exasperated, as if he's simply tired of the conversation. I can understand why though—Levi already explained a bit about Olivia's car accident last fall, and the drama in her relationship with Drew.

Olivia leads us that way, and I shoot Levi a quick reassuring look—he may smile back at me, but I can tell he's still tense.

There are a lot of people here, but somehow, it all feels natural—comfortable and relaxed, like they all belong.

Then, out of nowhere, a small blonde girl comes running from behind us and smacks into Levi.

I grin immediately recognizing Ellie from her pictures.

"ViVi! What are *you* doing here?!"

Levi swoops her up and looks at Cal. "Well, Ellie-Bellie, I want to introduce you to your cousin Cal."

Ellie looks at both of us, then back at Levi, puzzled. "Who's she?"

"That's Aubrey."

"You're really pretty! Mom says I can't get tattoos like Delta until I'm an adult, though." She starts scrambling out of Levi's arms, eyes on Cal, who's towering over her.

"Ben!" She shouts as she reaches for Cal's hand. "Benjamin Turner! We gots a new cousin!" she exclaims, pulling him toward the other side of the house.

Cal looks at Levi with wide eyes for help, but laughs as he follows behind her.

"I'll go help introduce them," Levi says, heading that way. "You okay?"

I nod, and he squeezes my hand as he walks away, a quiet reassurance.

Olivia grins, her arm still around me. "Come on, I'll introduce you to the bod squad."

"The what?" I ask, amused, but she only continues to smile nonchalantly.

"We've got Liam—he's no bark, all bite, but only to those who deserve it. Cooper's got the stache and will probably—no, definitely— try to hit on you. Leo—our aspiring politician slash actor. And Delta," she says, waving her hand at a guy covered in tattoos. "He's..."

She pauses, thinking, then Cooper pipes up, "the most average of us all!"

I can't help but giggle as Delta smacks him in the back of the head.

"I was gonna say our tatted Delta Force operator," she clarifies. "Him and Everett—who isn't here—were both in the Army."

Cooper's mustache twists lopsided. "Sure, Liv. Sure."

I glance at the last guy, who sits next to a beautiful girl with her eyes glued to her laptop, looking completely zoned out.

"And last but not least, we have Lincoln!" I recognize the name immediately—one I've heard in my talks with Levi, and the infamous email too.

Lincoln looks up, raising an eyebrow at me—a silent dare or test, I'm not sure.

I simply smile and reply, "Hi. I think you're actually one of the reasons I'm here—well, we're here."

"What do you mean?" Olivia asks first, tilting her head.

I clasp my hands if front of me to keep myself from shaking, but I swear every set of male eyes goes to them, as if they're reading my body language for lies. *Shit.*

"Right, so... I guess I should start," I say, my voice shaky. Before I can get any farther, Levi's arm wraps around my shoulders, pulling me close.

"Come on, let's sit," he says softly, guiding me toward the kitchen island. He turns the chairs so we're facing everyone. "Cal's good. He's over there playing Switch with the other kids."

When we sit, he takes my hand in his, squeezing gently.

"Think I should start?" he asks softly.

I nod, feeling most of my nerves melt away.

"Alright," Levi begins, voice steady. "The short version is that I dated Aubrey's sister, Sienna, about twelve years ago. We met on campus, things moved fast, and pretty soon, we found out she was pregnant. Shortly after, she had a pulmonary embolism, a blood clot that went straight to her lungs and cut off her oxygen supply. I found her on the floor of her apartment and rushed her to the hospital— but it was too late."

His voice tightens. "She died."

A hush falls over us. Olivia and Charlie gasp, hands flying to their mouths. I feel myself shrinking, knowing what's coming.

"Things got a little lost in the mix," Levi continues quietly. "I thought she was gone—"

"My mom told him she was dead," I cut in, voice shaking. "You don't have to sugarcoat it, Levi. She lied. Don't blame yourself for not knowing."

His lips curl into a small, almost grateful smile, and he nods once.

"So yeah," Levi continues, glancing back at the group. "Sienna was placed in a coma until Cal—" he hesitates, turning to look at me, sadness flickering in his eyes, and I realize we haven't talked about that part yet.

"The goal was to get him as close to full-term as possible, but he was born at 27 weeks. She had another blood clot, and the doctors decided he had a better chance of surviving outside of her," I fill in for him, eyes fixed on his, only they don't reveal anything. It's like he's processing it, imagining the scenario in his head.

"Wow. That's kind of incredible—for Cal, obviously," Charlie quickly covers, and I smile at her. "He was tiny, but a little fighter."

They all look at me, some with sympathy, others still reserved.

"So, how'd you come up with the name Cal?" Olivia asks, studying Levi and me like she knows something, but I'm not quite sure what.

I smile despite feeling a little left out of their silent conversation—picking Cal's name was honestly the one confident decision I'd made during all the chaos. "That was one thing Sienna said when I asked her if she wanted a boy or girl—'A little boy named Cal.'"

Levi squeezes my hand again, and I notice his smile widen as he mouths, "Thank you," silently. I feel that strange, uncomfortable sense of being left out of something still, but I push it aside.

Charlie breaks the moment, changing the subject. "If Cal was born prematurely, what happened after that?" she asks, standing in front of Hayes as she rocks her sleeping baby.

I pick up from there. "Yeah. After that, my mom moved us to Tacoma. I was young and naive—no excuses, really—but I believed her when she said Levi didn't want anything to do with Sienna or Cal."

"She pretty much raised Cal," Levi says proudly, though I can see the skepticism still lingering on his friends' faces.

"You never tried to reach out, though?" Maisie asks, her voice sharper, more accusatory than curious.

Levi tenses beside me, and I subtly squeeze his hand, trying to offer comfort. I'd expected this, maybe not tonight, but I knew his friends would have questions.

"Nope," I reply, voice dripping with sass. "Why would I beg some man to be in the best kid I know's life?"

I soften slightly, looking at Levi, and adding, "No offense."

"None taken." He grins, almost as if he's relieved I didn't back down.

Then he looks directly at Maisie. "Aubrey was *fourteen* when Sienna died. I think I said 'hi' to her once, in the driveway, when she was walking out to a friend's house. She. didn't. know. me."

"I definitely didn't," I confirm. "Again, it's not an excuse. It's just the truth. I believed my mom—until—" I glance at Lincoln, "—until I got that email."

Once again, Olivia gasps loudly. "What email?" she insists looking between the two of us and then throwing a scolding look back at Drew.

Lincoln shrinks back, glancing from Hayes to Olivia to me. Hayes looks to Drew, then Levi, then back to Lincoln. Suddenly, I feel like I'm in that Spider-Man meme—everyone pointing fingers at each other, and no one saying a word.

Hayes sighs deeply and begins filling in the gaps. "Lincoln's been digging into Mitchell and Walton—every scrap he can find from the last twenty years."

I nod silently, feeling the weight of it all. I don't know much about Mitchell and Walton, other than what Levi has explained about what happened to Isla. That, in itself, is enough to know they're truly terrible men—and the fact that they held any power is downright frightening. The podcaster in me, though, is desperate to know more—to dig like Lincoln and uncover every disgraceful thing they did to out them.

Lincoln continues, "I may or may not have read some emails, dating back as far as twenty years. One from Rosa Dubrow, during a routine divorce—she cleaned out her husband. And another case, very tight lipped, most emails only to arrange phone calls—except for one. In that one, he congratulated her on her baby."

"Cal," Charlie quietly prompts, and we all nod.

"So, Rosa, is your mom?" Maisie asks, and all eyes fix on me.

All I do is nod in response, feeling like a tennis ball of emotion is clogging up my throat suddenly.

"She used those assholes to get legal custody of Cal?" Maisie presses, her voice almost accusing.

I only nod again, my gaze drifting away, fixing on a spot on the wall. Tears begin to sting my eyes, and it takes all I have to blink them away.

"Okay," Charlie offers and it's almost like I can hear the support in that one word. "So—" she prods, but still her voice kind, "what happened after you saw that email?"

"Uhm," I say with a half-hearted laugh. "I spiraled."

"Rightfully so," Olivia offers sympathetically.

"Then? Then, I Googled Levi—found out everything I could about him—and most of you, if I'm being honest."

"Aw, that's kind of sweet," Olivia smiles.

"Yeah, well, Cal caught me once, thinking Levi was Dan from the memorial,"

"Oh, shit," Charlie says, eyes wide.

"Pretty much," I reply.

Levi begins to smile, his real smile, and he adds, "And then they showed up on my doorstep a few weeks ago."

Olivia gasps looking between the two of us, "You've been here for weeks?"

"No, no," I quickly correct. "That was just a weekend trip, but we've stayed in touch since. Cal had to finish school, and now we're here for a few days."

"And Rosa?" Maisie asks, her tone edged with suspicion. "She's—?"

"In Florida. She's been a traveling nurse for a while," I reply, glancing at Lincoln. It's clear on his face that he already knows this. I knew he was sharp, could find out anything, but now I'm starting to wonder what else he knows and isn't saying.

"She's okay with Levi knowing about Cal?" Maisie asks, but again it feels like an accusation.

"Not exactly," I admit.

"She doesn't know. She's trying to move Cal to Florida." Levi's tone is calm but firm.

"So that's why you're here," Maisie alleges, her voice heavy with distrust.

"I—" I start, but Levi cuts in smoothly.

"Maisie," he almost sounds like he's condemning her, "it's not like that."

She softens slightly when she looks at him, but only just. Then her eyes flick back to me, and I have to remind myself— they're both battling some deep-rooted issues that have all come to the surface at once. For years, they hid their secrets together. Now, it's all out in the open, and somehow, they're the ones fighting it out.

"Levi, the timing..." she begins.

"Does it really matter how long it takes to right a wrong?" Levi counters, his tone sharp and accusatory, glancing toward Ethan, who wraps his arms protectively around Maisie.

The room falls into a tense silence, thick with charges unspoken—like a standoff, each of them staring each other down.

Finally, Ethan breaks the stillness. "If there's one thing this group is good at," he says, voice steady, "it's forgiving and moving forward."

Maisie looks at me briefly, then up at Ethan, and nods.

Feeling like I still need to justify myself, I take a breath. "Look, I know showing up after twelve years isn't ideal—but I'm not here with ulterior motives. I'm the one facing losing him. If Levi fights for custody, I might lose Cal. If my mom moves him to Florida, I lose him altogether. He's been with me every single day since he was born—every damn day."

Levi nods, then adds, "Aubrey didn't go to a regular high school. She switched to online so she could help with Cal."

"You were fourteen?" Hayes asks, eyebrows raised. "That's younger than most teen moms."

I nod. "It was my decision. I was grieving Sienna too. I begged my mom to let me stay home, and that was a constant battle. She did something wrong, there's no denying that, but she's not a bad person. And I get it—there are things you may never understand or forgive—but Cal and I have had a good life."

Levi offers a soft smile. "Cal's at one of the best private schools in Tacoma."

"He is. We've never wanted for anything. That doesn't mean it's fair. And I'm sure you—like Levi and Pops—feel betrayed," I add, voice thickening.

Charlie's jaw drops. "Pops knows?"

"Their first day in town, he was at my house," Levi laughs. "He got the whole story before I even did."

"What do we do now?" Olivia asks quietly.

"That's why I called Hayes and scheduled a meeting for

Monday morning," Levi replies. "We don't really know what's going to happen, but we don't want to go in guns blazing. Neither of us wants Cal dragged into a huge custody battle."

I nod in agreement, "but we also don't think he should move to Florida."

"Would he want to move here," Hayes asks this time.

I glance to Levi before nodding, "he told me on the drive here that he would rather live here than Florida—or Tacoma."

"And what about you?" Charlie asks.

"I'd love to move back to this area," I say genuinely. Then I look to Olivia. "If you have any rentals available anytime soon, would you let me know?"

She grins. "We'll find something for you both, no problem."

Levi tenses next to me, his eyes bouncing between us, and a rush of nerves overwhelms me, like I said something wrong.

"Alright," Hayes starts, "so let's keep the meeting for Monday. We can brainstorm some ideas on where to go next. We've got a former client who does family law—I'll give him a call and see if he's available for a video call."

"Thanks, man," Levi says, standing and shaking Hayes's hand, who then pulls him into a hug.

"Whatever you guys need," Drew adds, walking over and putting a hand on Levi's shoulder. "Call anytime."

I nod, standing too. "Thank you all so much. Again, I'm really sorry to crash this whole night. Somehow we turned it all to about us." I look directly at Maisie, hoping to convey to her specifically, "but I appreciate your graciousness about everything."

Maisie doesn't even look at me; instead, she's looking at her feet. I glance up to Ethan, who gives me a sympathetic smile and nods. "At least it got our minds off everything that happened before."

Olivia comes over, wrapping her arms around me as best she can with her pregnant belly. "Agreed—and like Hayes said, there's never a bad time to learn about new family. Especially when they're as great as you and Cal seem to be."

Chapter Twenty-Four

Aubrey

My phone dings, waking me from my deep sleep. Last night was intense and I went to bed emotionally exhausted. Levi's family was great, a little guarded at first but by the time we left, I felt accepted—by most anyway. Then, we got home and Levi and I recapped everything, expressing our own worries to each other, and it was so cathartic that I went to bed feeling raw but heard. Levi said he's fully in—for Cal and me—and last night I believed him. *So why did I wake up today with an emotional hangover that has the doubt creeping back in?*

I groggily reach for my phone when it dings again, squinting at the bright screen in the darkness of my room. My mothers name appears, and I can't help but groan.

MOM:

> Cal's not responding to me.

> Where are you? I don't like this secretive business Aubrey.

I can't help but roll my eyes, "secretive business" as if she hasn't been keeping MAJOR secrets for Cal's entire life.

My phone starts ringing, and I want to ignore it, but I also know that will only cause her to panic.

"Hi, mom." I answer

"Aubrey, where are you? You go off on some crazy roadtrip without even telling me and now you're going out on a lake and wont even tell me where on earth you are?"

Before I can answer she keeps going, "Cal hasn't talked to me in two days. I tried to call, and he didn't answer. I've sent multiple texts and he's only 'thumbs upped' them. What is going on with that kid? He's never treated me this way."

If it weren't for the genuine concern in her voice, I probably would have gone off on her. Instead I lead with a calm tone, and say, "mom, you're trying to move him across the country—to a place he's barely visited, and doesn't know anyone. He's upset."

"But—it's for his benefit. Florida is wonderful, the schools—"

"Mom, he's twelve! He doesn't care about the schools. He cares about moving away from me." *Something you obviously don't understand.*

"Aubrey, we've talked about this. You need—"

"No, I don't actually. I'm happy with my life. I love Cal—raising him, and being his support person. You say you're only thinking about me and Cal, but this is a selfish decision mom. So yeah, Cal's ignoring you because he's upset. You'll have to live with that, or back off and let him stay with me."

"In Tacoma? Why are you so set on staying there?" she demands.

"I'm not, Mom. But if I choose to move away from Tacoma, it's because Cal also wants to. He has just as much vote as I do, and while you may not see it that way, his happiness and well-being are my top priorities."

"Aubrey Dubrow, his happiness and well-being have always been my top priority! Don't you for a second think otherwise." *Says the woman who took a traveling position at work and has been gone for the last two years.*

"You asked why he isn't talking to you and I explained it. You can be pissed all you want, but that's the reality."

"Have him call me," she demands before hanging up the phone.

There goes my fucking morning.

I know I need to shake off that call and put on a happy face for Cal and Levi, so I start with a hot shower, giving myself a little extra time on my skincare routine and applying some makeup. We may be about to spend the day at the lake, but I still want to look nice.

By the time I feel mostly put together, I realize I haven't heard the guys in the house once.

As I search through the house, I open the front door and catch sight of Levi by the truck. He's arms loaded with two paddle boards, and I see one already in the back. The two he's holding gleam—new, pristine, untouched—while the third looks a little worn, its colors faded enough to tell it's seen a few summers. He has that all-American surfer boy look—sun-bleached blonde hair tousled from the breeze, muscles rippling under his tank top as he maneuvers the boards into the bed of the truck. He almost seems like he belongs on some endless coastline poster.

He notices me and grins wide, that signature bright smile—

carefree yet confident all at once. "The water will still be a bit cold," he says, voice relaxed, "but I was too excited to wait."

I blink, a little confused. "You bought these?"

He laughs, that easy, genuine sound that makes it hard to believe he's even real. "Well, yeah. You and Cal need your own for this summer." He pauses, eyes drifting over the boards as if imagining us out on the water. "You know, instead of renting every time."

For a second, I hesitate, staring at the boards like maybe the question shouldn't even be asked. I feel that familiar flicker of doubt—second-guessing what I need, what I deserve. Then I ask it anyway, voice trying to sound casual. "How much do I owe you?"

He looks genuinely taken aback, blinking like I've just tossed a pebble into his calm surface. "Nothing, Aubs. It's a gift. A welcome-to-town gift."

I nod slowly, trying to process it—the gesture, the kindness behind it, and the simplicity of him offering so freely. He's one of the most sincere guys I've ever met, and his generosity catches me off guard in the best way. It's a reminder that not everyone has ulterior motives; sometimes people are just genuinely kind. That's why I went to bed last night feeling reassured and confident about being here.

Cal walks out from the garage, carrying a cooler with beach towels on top. "Dad! Did you mean this one?" He's already dressed in board shorts and a tank top similar to Levi's.

Levi beams—his signature bright smile—when Cal calls him "Dad," and he nods. "Yep, that's the perfect size for some drinks and lunch."

"What *are* we taking for lunch?" Cal asks, and I love the simplicity of this conversation. It makes it easy to let go of the heaviness I just had with my mom. *Cal's happy here.*

Levi answers, talking about this little market on the way out to Sparks Lake that has the best deli sandwiches.

I turn, heading back inside to finish getting ready, grabbing my swimsuit and sunscreen. I can't wait to spend the day relaxing by the lake with my two favorite guys. *Two favorite guys.* Just that thought makes my heart flutter. *One kiss and I'm already putting him on the same level as Cal.*

By the time we pull up to the lake, Levi is already in full-on tour guide mode. He's talking about every good thing in Central Oregon—the endless summers, the quiet mornings, the way the sun hits the mountains just right. It's like he's become a personal spokesman for Three Sisters; a waxing poetic about small-town charm and outdoor life you can't find anywhere else. I can't help but laugh at how hard he's trying to convince us to move here, like it's some secret I've missed out on all these years. *Which, okay, I really have.*

I mentioned it briefly last night, but Cal already made up his mind. He's jumping headfirst—just like his dad—completely sold on the idea of moving in, trading the city for dirt roads and mountain air.

Meanwhile, I'm the one hesitating.

I'm caught in a mental tug-of-war. I love the idea of new beginnings, but part of me is nervous—about messing it all up, about moving too fast. Fears I didn't even realize I had start to creep in. *Is it for Cal or for me? Is it because of Levi and me, or because I worry it might all turn out to be a fairy tale?*

Levi's voice pulls me back, rambling about the best places to eat, the trails to hike, and the quiet coves where we could paddle until sunset. I listen, nodding along, trying to hide how much I'm overthinking everything inside. Because deep down, I know Cal's already all in. And maybe—that's what I need to be brave enough to do too.

We all hop out of the truck, and my jaw nearly drops at the

view stretched before us. The lake sparkles and shimmers under the bright sun, like a mirror reflecting the clear blue sky. There are only a few people out on the water, scattered enough that it feels almost like our own private paradise. I take a slow breath, standing there mesmerized, staring at the quiet beauty. Levi points out the South Sister and Broken Top, and my eyes follow his finger, feeling as if I could reach out and touch the mountains. They tower majestically over us, yet they feel close enough to touch.

I stand there a moment longer, soaking it all in—lost in the stillness and the stunning view. Then I finally turn away, walking over to the driver's side of the truck. I want to peel off my shirt and shorts, stuff them into the truck, and get ready. As I reach for my tank top, I feel Levi's gaze shift to me.

I catch him staring, eyes roaming over my bikini, and a blush hits my cheeks before I even realize it. It's quick, but I can feel his gaze lingering just a second longer than casual, making my skin tingle. Then he grins, tossing his head back, eyes closed, before busily grabbing the paddle boards, pretending he didn't just get caught.

Instead of looking away like I should, I can't stop staring at him. The way he carries two huge boards down to the water's edge like it's nothing, the muscles in his arms flexing with each step. He sets them down with ease, and I tear my eyes away quickly before I get caught myself. But when I look up, Cal is already staring at me.

He's eyeing me with a deadpan look, but I notice him glancing at Levi, then at me, then back again. Our eyes meet, and—shit—he starts laughing loudly, the kind of laugh that makes his whole chest shake. "You're drooling, Aunnie," he teases, pointing at me with a crooked grin.

I suck in a sharp breath, heat rushing to my cheeks. "Cal!" I hiss, trying to cover the flush creeping across my face. But he only laughs even harder, his amusement lighting up his face.

Levi finally comes over, holding three bright life jackets. He hands the first one to Cal, who accepts it and heads toward the water, all serious now. Then Levi turns to me, holding out the last one. I start to protest, opening my mouth to say I don't need one, but Cal shoots me a look, and I catch Levi's steady, no-nonsense gaze.

"As much as I want to stare at you in only that bikini all day," Levi says quietly, voice serious, "we don't mess with water safety. Even the strongest swimmers can run into trouble, and the lives that could be saved just by wearing one of these..." He trails off, handing it to me, his voice suddenly soft as if lost in a memory.

I nod slowly, letting his words sink in and soften the stubborn part of me that wanted to push back. It suddenly feels kind of silly to argue, but there's a quiet reassurance in knowing he cares enough to remind me. It's comforting—I like feeling protected, even over something as simple as a life jacket. I slide it on, feeling a bit lighter and more cared for, as we spend the rest of the day together in the water.

Chapter Twenty-Five

Levi

Aubrey in that dress is going to be the death of me.

She looks stunning as we walk up the stairs of Olivia's building, the one she shares with the EFSC guys. It's one of those summertime dresses that is flowy and light, the white complementing her sun-kissed skin and carefree smile. Her tattoos peeking out from the thin straps add an edge to her overall look, making her even more captivating—like I could stare at them all day, tracing each one with my eyes.

She looks perfect, yet I nearly asked her to change this morning. Not for any other reason than pure selfishness, because we're about to walk into a room full of single guys, and she looks like a temptation worth fighting over.

I didn't say anything, though. I'm not a controlling asshole and I know these guys aren't pigs. They've got enough respect for the situation I'm in, or at least normally they do.

The dress though, is dangerous, and the confidence she has wearing it is both intimidating and alluring.

"Think the kids are having fun with Pops?" she asks nervously, snapping me out of my fantasy.

My dad picked up Cal about an hour ago to take him, Ellie, and Ben fishing at one of the ponds he used to bring Dan and me to when we were their age. It was one of the few things I remember doing with my dad; he was always working, but during the summer, he'd take a random day off and take us out there—letting us fish, explore, and just be kids.

I smile at her reassuringly and say, "Definitely—he spoils those kids rotten. I have no doubt Cal is living his best life snacking on chips and drinking sodas from the bank."

She swallows hard, looking forward towards the second floor, and I realize it's not my dad and Cals she worried about—it's this meeting.

I reach out, stopping her, my hand covering where hers is resting on her arm.

"Hey, we're together in this. Whatever advice they give and whether we take it or not—we decide together."

Her eyes soften as she looks back at me, a grateful smile playing on her lips. "Sorry—it's just a lot."

I give her a reassuring squeeze before moving my hand to the center of her back as we finish walking up the stairs.

The EFSC office is the first door up the steps, the rest of the office has glass wall partitions and you can see into the other offices.

I turn, looking toward Olivia and Charlie's office behind me. Olivia's standing there, one hand on her belly, as she points to her desk talking to Charlie and Isla.

"Come on," I say guiding Aubrey around the railing toward Olivia's office. Maybe a little feminine energy will help ease Aubrey's nerves before the meeting.

Charlie's holding August, bouncing him gently in the wrap around her chest. She's the first to look up, waving with her free hand that isn't supporting August. Olivia, closer to us, turns and a huge smile lights up her face as she waddles toward us.

To our right is the "game room," which has couches, a giant table mostly used for Legos, and a TV mounted on the wall. Olivia designed it for the kids so they'd have a space to play while she worked.

"See that bean bag chair?" I say, pointing at the oversized, brightly colored bean bag in the corner.

Aubrey nods, glancing back at me. "I helped deliver August on it."

Her eyes widen. "You're joking?"

Olivia laughs at what I said. "We cleaned it, don't worry!" She hugs Aubrey first, then turns to me and gives a knowing look. "Hi, guys!"

Isla appears behind her, introducing herself to Aubrey, so I decide to ignore Olivia.

"It's so nice to meet you, Aubrey! I'm Isla," she says, tossing her braid over her shoulder. Isla has been working for Olivia for quite some time—nearly as long as Charlie—and it feels like the trio has been working together forever. Isla's warm smile seems to put Aubrey at ease, and I'm glad I chose to make this pit stop before going into the lion's den.

"Hi! This place is incredible," Aubrey says, glancing around.

"Well, it was before all that toxic male energy moved in," Charlie announces loudly, winking across the room. I glance over Aubrey's head to see Hayes walking out.

"Don't even start, Sunshine," he says playfully, stepping around us to kiss her on the forehead.

He then turns to us. "Y'all ready to start this meeting? The attorney I mentioned is available in about thirty minutes to go over the details, but I'd like to hear your thoughts first."

"Ready when you are," Aubrey says, grabbing her tattoo and giving it a firm squeeze.

We head into the conference room of the EFSC office,

where Lincoln and Drew are already seated. There's a huge wooden table that looks like it could fit at least twenty people.

"Hey," Drew says, standing and smiling as he gestures for us to take a seat. Lincoln nods, his hand resting on the table, giving a small wave.

"Hey, guys. Thanks for meeting with us," I say as Aubrey and I settle into our seats across from them.

Hayes sits on the other side of Drew, and I can tell they're both trying to keep this casual.

"Anytime. So—obviously we don't know much on our end but we are happy to help in anyway we can."

"What do you know?" Aubrey asks him confidently.

Lincoln starts, "That's more my area. I'm assuming Levi filled you in on what happened with Mitchell and Walton?"

We both nod, and he continues, "The FBI technically took over the case, but I've been doing my own research in my free-time."

Hayes and Drew both give a short laugh, as if they find Lincoln's dedication amusing.

"By research, he means completely not legal hacking," Drew adds with a smirk.

"But that stays in the office, and will be denied if anyone asks," Hayes chimes in seriously, but I know him well enough to detect a hint of amusement in his voice.

Lincoln shrugs, "Anyway, as I mentioned the other night. Your mom and Marcus Mitchell had been emailing for a few months prior to the divorce proceedings." He reaches for a stack of papers, sliding them over. Aubrey scans them without touching them, then reaches into her bag and pulls out her own folders. "I already have all these."

Lincoln nods, impressed. "Anything else you have?"

She shrugs, handing over the files. "It's the only information

I found in my mom's room. I don't know what any of it means, but it seems like you may already have it all."

Drew smiles. "Lincoln is known for his thoroughness. He'll be able to make sense of it all." Lincoln looks away quickly before saying, "I'll do my best to connect the dots."

I look to Hayes, feeling the energy shift and he gives me one slight head shake, as if to say, "I'll tell you later."

Hayes's phone rings and he nods, "The attorney," he says before pointing toward the screen as Lincoln hits some buttons on his computer and suddenly the call is coming through the tv.

"Mr. Diamond," Hayes says in greeting as a clean cut man wearing a suit and glasses appears on the screen.

"Gentleman, miss— how are you all today?"

"Good, good," Hayes says leading the conversation. "How's the family? Everyone doing well?"

Mr. Diamond nods, almost graciously, "They're all doing damn fine. Thank you again for helping with that little problem last year."

Hayes smiles, "No problem. So—we're actually here for advice and potentially to use your services—if Aubrey and Levi see fit, that is."

Mr Diamond turns to us, "Nice to officially meet you both. Hayes filled me in a bit on the basics, but we both agreed waiting until this meeting would be best."

I nod, "Thank you. I appreciate that—I think I'd like to start out by saying that we want to make this as easy as possible on my son, Cal. We're trying to avoid a huge custody battle where he gets dragged through the mud."

"That's always the goal," he acknowledges, softly. "Why don't you explain a little more on how we got into this situation."

The next twenty minutes, Aubrey and I take turns sharing the timeline of how we got here.

"Alright," he begins, his voice smooth and deliberate. "From what you've told me, this is a complicated case—fraud, a hidden birth, and custody all tangled up with Rosa's actions and possibly others'. It's not impossible. In fact, I think you have a very strong case—so long as we approach this methodically and show the judge that we're focused on what's best for Cal."

I nod, trying to absorb everything, feeling a mixture of hope and worry coursing through me.

"First," he says, "you need to establish your paternity legally. In Oregon, that means genetic testing. We can request a court order to have Cal's DNA tested. Once paternity is confirmed, you'll have standing as a legal parent, which is crucial for filing for custody or visitation rights."

He pauses, making sure I'm following. I nod again, my heart pounding.

"Now, regarding Rosa," he continues, "her actions to hide the birth and list herself as the mother could be challenged legally—if we can prove it was done under false pretenses or with fraudulent intent. Oregon law allows courts to amend birth records in cases where fraud or mistake is involved. If we can demonstrate that she misled authorities or acted unlawfully when she claimed custody, that could weaken her case."

"So, I could request a court to revise the birth record?" I ask, trying to keep my voice steady.

"Exactly," he confirms. "It's a process—sometimes complex, but entirely possible, especially when there's evidence of deception. This isn't just about paperwork; it's about establishing your genuine legal relationship with Cal."

He leans forward slightly. "In terms of custody, the court's primary concern is what's in Cal's best interest. That includes your involvement, your ability to provide stability, and your relationship with him over the years. Considering you have limited contact with him before last month, it's not in your favor. However, because of the unique relationship with his aunt and her involvement in his upbringing, the court may consider granting her full custody and you visitation.

"But what about Rosa? We aren't seeking any legal repercussions," I ask.

He shrugs, "I'm not sure, it could be picked up by the D.A. especially if we show her actions deprived Cal of knowing his biological parent or interfered with your rights. Oregon courts tend to favor stability and your ability to provide a loving environment."

I chew on that, feeling a flicker of hope but also dread about what's ahead.

"And what about Sienna?" Aubrey asks, "Is there anyway that the court can change his birth records to reflect her as his mother?"

He pauses thoughtfully. "I don't see why that would be an issue, assuming they're able to verify Sienna's biological relationship to Cal. It would likely require a legal process, but it's definitely a possibility." Aubrey nods, looking relieved for the first time since this started.

"The biggest challenge will be confronting the deception and convincing the court that you're the person who should be guiding Cal's future. That means gathering all evidence—your involvement and any communication—and Aubrey will need to have a testimony about your role."

I feel myself clenching my fists, trying to hold onto hope.

"Lastly," Mr. Diamond says softly, "I recommend you document everything—your involvement with Cal, your interactions, any evidence of the fraudulent birth—so we have everything we need. It's going to be a fight, but I believe we can make a strong case."

I nod, feeling a mix of gratitude and anxiety. "Thank you, I appreciate that. We'll get back to you after we have some time to discuss, if that's alright with you."

"Not a problem. Hayes has my number, and I'll be available whenever you're ready to move forward."

"I'll let you know, thanks again."

Lincoln ends the call and then stands up, grabbing his computer. "I'll let you talk; I'll be in my office if you need me."

Hayes and Drew remain seated, heavy with the weight of the conversation.

"I guess the next step is for you two to figure out how you want to proceed."

I look over at Aubrey again—her face relaxed, but eyes a little distant, like she's thinking about everything the attorney said. I want to reassure her and tell her it's going to be okay, that I'll do whatever it takes to keep her and Cal protected. But I also can't guarantee that everything will work out perfectly. So instead, I offer a small smile and a nod of support before turning back to Hayes and Drew.

"I think no matter what, we need to establish legal paternity. There's no doubt in my mind that he's mine, but we need to make sure everything is official and in writing for his protection as well."

Drew agrees, "Not to be morbid, but if anything happened to you, I'm assuming you'd want Cal to be your beneficiary. You need to make sure all the legalities are in place to ensure he receives everything you would want him to have."

Hayes nods in agreement, adding, "Aubrey, you made a good point. It isn't fair to Sienna's memory that she isn't recognized legally as Cal's mother. You either, Levi, but that was a given. I think this goes beyond a custody battle."

I feel a sense of determination building within me; they're right. Rosa may have had good intentions in raising Cal, but it's time for us to make sure he is legally recognized as my son and Sienna's.

Aubrey looks up, her shoulders having all but deflated as she says, "Will you let Mr Diamond know that we want to start the legal proceedings?"

Hayes looks at her sympathetically. "Are you sure? You can sleep on it for a day or two."

She shakes her head quickly. "No—it's long overdue." Then, suddenly, she wipes her face, and I see more tears immediately falling.

I reach out to her, but she's already standing. "Will you excuse me? I need—" she doesn't finish before turning and practically running out the door.

"Thanks, guys," I say, already rising to follow her but hesitating, not wanting to be rude.

"Well don't just stand there, you idiot," Drew huffs.

"Go comfort your girl," Hayes adds.

I don't have time to think about the fact that they read the situation so clearly, instead I barrel out the door and down the stairs after her.

Only when I throw open the front door, she's nowhere in sight.

Chapter Twenty-Six

Aubrey

I practically threw myself down the stairs as I ran—the only reason I didn't fall was because I had a death grip on the railing.

As soon as I was outside, I felt like I could breathe again and pressed my back against the brick wall.

The rough edges felt warm under my skin as I worked to calm myself down. I couldn't stop crying in that office, but the adrenaline rush from leaving must have helped because I already feel a bit better.

Then, in the same frantic fashion as me, the doors fly open, and Levi comes barreling out, his eyes wild with panic—only he doesn't stop. He's at least four feet out the door, his head whipping around as if I vanished into thin air.

"Aubrey!" he yells, panic so evident I can't help but laugh at the situation.

"I'm right here."

He spins so fast he nearly stumbles, relief flooding his face as he locks eyes with me. "Fuck, you scared me," he breathes, arms going out to wrap around me.

"Sorry," I mumble, feeling guilty. "I didn't mean to bail up there. I was about two seconds from freaking out, and it was like the glass walls were closing in."

He chuckles softly. "It's okay, baby. That conversation was intense, and agreeing to legal action was a huge step."

"I know—and now the next step is even scarier. I have to tell Cal." I admit, feeling that familiar dread settle inside me again.

"We—we have to tell him. I want to be there, to explain why it's important to me that his birth records are changed. I want him to understand the reason I'm doing this."

I take a deep breath and slowly exhale. "He's going to hate her."

"I won't say anything about Rosa—I know it's hard to believe, but I don't want him to hate your mom. You said it yourself, she gave him an incredible life. Two things can be true: she screwed me over while setting him up for success. I will never place my anger toward her onto him. It's—not the same, because there wasn't a divorce or an ex-wife involved in this scenario. But I have a buddy whose ex-wife is a real... character. As awful as she is to him, he always says, 'I love my kids more than I hate her.' I think it applies here; I love Cal more than I hate your mom. I won't speak ill of her to him, I promise."

"I trust you," I finally admit. His hand brushes down my face, cupping my cheek, and he offers a gentle, acknowledging smile.

"You know, your eyes are really pretty when you cry—they almost turn golden."

"Levi!" I scold, though I could bask in his compliments all day.

"It's true," he says softly, grabbing my hand and leading me toward his truck, opening the door for me. "Come on, let's go talk to Cal."

Cal arrives home about an hour later, swinging the door open with that familiar energy of his. Pops follows behind him, both of them grinning wide enough to light up the room. I can tell they've had a good time—Pops looks like they just won some trophy for catching the biggest fish, and Cal's cheeks are practically glowing.

They see us standing in the kitchen, and Pops says, "We had the best time. Didn't catch a single thing, though."

Cal laughs, and the two exchange a look that's full of mischief and camaraderie. "Got the other two kids in the car. Gotta take 'em back to Olivia's," he says, giving us a quick wave. "See y'all later!"

Cal plops onto the arm of the couch after grabbing a bag of chips, and I can't stop the automatic eye roll. He's definitely picked that one up from Levi—probably forever mimicking his dad.

I clear my throat gently and start the conversation, trying to keep my voice steady. "So, there's something your dad and I need to talk to you about."

Cal nods, leaning back. "Brooo-no. I already heard the birds and bees, and I don't want to hear *anything* about you two birding and bee-ing."

My jaw drops. *Did he really just say that?* Before I can respond, Levi bursts into laughter, collapsing onto the couch, keeled over and clutching his stomach.

"Cal, that's not—no," I start, but Levi grins, mumbling under his breath, "yet."

"Seriously," I say, shaking my head, "it's about the whole moving to Florida with grandma thing."

Cal shrugs, looking unconcerned. "Yeah, I don't want to do that."

I take a deep breath. "Well, there's more. We found out Levi isn't listed on your birth certificate."

Cal slows his chewing, looking between us with a confused frown. "So I gotta spit in a tube or something so they can make sure I'm his?"

I glance at Levi, then back at him. "Kinda. The state needs to verify paternity so Levi can be officially listed. And, since grandma's listed as your biological mom, we're thinking about fighting so that your real mom gets recognized."

He nods slowly. "Sure. So... what does this have to do with Florida? Are you thinking that if Levi gets verified, he can get custody and then we can move here?"

Again, I look at Levi—*how does he seem to know all this?* Levi answers before I can.

"It's a little more multifaceted than fighting for just custody," he says softly, "but basically, yes, that would help. I want to make sure that no matter what, you know you're mine. And you're loved."

Cal shrugs. "Already know that."

Levi nods, tilting his head. "I know you do, but unfortunately, Oregon doesn't always see it that way. I need to file for legal paternity—and I'd also like to fight for custody. It's going to be a long process, and your grandma won't be happy about it."

Cal looks at me, eyes searching. "Are you cool with it?"

"I am," I reply honestly. "I think Levi's a good dad, and I believe you'd be happy living here."

His eyes narrow suspiciously. "What about you?"

"I think I'd be happy here, too," I admit, then quickly add, "though I did ask Olivia to look for a rental. Moving in right away might be too soon, but I'll be close—you could go between places."

I notice Levi stiffen next to me, but he stays quiet, just watching us.

"Cool," Cal says, stretching. "That makes sense with dad's shifts, right?"

Levi seems to consider it for a moment before folding his arms. "I'm still holding out for both of you to move here."

Cal grins mischievously, then dumps the rest of the chip bag straight into his mouth. "Gonna shower. Let me know when we're heading north to pack our bags and all that."

I look over at Levi, who's grinning like he's about to crack up. "You sure he's not really fifteen?"

I shrug, keeping it light. "I don't know—I wasn't there for the bird'ing and bee'ing of his conception."

Levi lets out a loud laugh, then, unexpectedly, nearly tackles me into a hug. He kisses everywhere on my face except my lips, still grinning wildly.

Looking down at me, he says, "That went good, right?"

"Too good," I confirm with a small, breathless laugh. There was zero hesitation on Cal's side and whether that's because of his confidence in Levi or that he knows no matter what I won't leave him, I don't know. I do wish I was on his level though—instead, I still only feel worried that I'm fucking it all up.

Chapter Twenty-Seven

Aubrey

The sound of trucks on gravel pulls my attention to the window. Three trucks in a convoy down Levi's road.

"Levi!" I try not to yell, but I can feel my heart racing.

"What?" he says, nearly running to me.

He looks out the window. "Oh, it's—" he pauses, his eyes narrowing. "Well, it's the guys."

"What guys?"

"Uh, Hayes in front, then Ethan, then Lincoln."

"Why are they here?"

"That, I don't know." We step outside, and I feel like a lead weight has settled in my stomach. I grip my arm, squeezing hard.

Hayes is the first out of his truck. "We're kidnapping you and Cal!"

Ethan slams his door. "Can we not use the 'k' word, asshole..."

"Right, my bad. We're, uh, transporting you to a much funner place for about three hours."

Cal steps out next to me.

Everett leans out the passenger side of Hayes's truck. "Get in, loser. We're going shopping!"

Cal and I both chuckle, but Levi throws me a side eye. Before I can say anything, Cal's grin widens.

"Mean Girls, Dad."

"See, Drew! Even the newest member of the pack gets it!"

Drew throws him another confused look, asking "the pack?"

"The wolf pack, awooooo!"

"Stop asking questions, dipshit," Hayes admonishes Drew, and I can't help but laugh at the chaos unfolding in front of me.

"So where we going?" Cal yells to them, already clearly excited.

Ben's head pops out from the other side of Ethan's truck. "Come on, Cal! You're riding with us! We're going bowling!" And then I hear from the furthest truck as Cooper yells, "Boys' night, boys' night!"

Levi looks at me, then at Cal, but Cal's already walking down the steps.

"Is it—?"

"Don't you dare even ask, Levi Turner." His grin widens, and I feel like I just won the lottery. I'd never say no to him and Cal having a 'boys' night.'

"Thanks, babe," he says, kissing my cheek quickly before taking off after Cal, and I yell, "You two have fun!"

Cal turns as he gets to Ethan's truck, and when I see the grin on his face, it's like my soul finally sees what it needed to. No matter what fight my mom brings, Cal belongs here.

"Hey, Aubrey!" Drew yells from Hayes's truck, and I look at him. "Girls' night at my house. If you're not there in the next twenty, you can expect a handful of girls on your porch dragging you out."

My face must blanch because Hayes yells, "They've got booze and Chinese food!"

"Oh, I—"

Then Drew, smiling, yells, "Be careful of the desserts, though! Liv's been experimenting, and they're not all hits."

My phone dings from my pocket. I pull it out to see a call from Levi. He's sitting in the front passenger seat of Ethan's truck.

"You don't have to go, but Hayes wasn't kidding when he said the girls will probably show up here."

"You don't think I'd be intruding?"

"Not at all. Go have fun. Have some drinks, and I'll drive you home after bowling."

"You don't want to drink?"

"Nah, you'll probably need it more than me tonight."

"That bad?" I ask.

"It'll be an interrogation for sure, but stick by Liv and Isla."

"Fine. Send me the address? I could probably find it again, but..."

"On it. And if it gets too bad, just text me, and I'll be right there to rescue you."

We end the call, and I look around Levi's kitchen for something to bring so I don't show up empty-handed. I find two bottles of wine in the pantry and examine them. They look fancy enough, but hopefully not too fancy, and I decide to grab them, knowing they'll come in handy during the interrogation. I quickly slip them into my bag before heading out the door for the short drive.

I try to think of the last time I hung out with friends and realize it's probably been since before Cal was born. Of course, I've hung around his friends' parents at birthday parties and school events, but it's not the same as having a real spill-the-tea session. Besides Molly, I don't even have real friends — and I haven't seen her in person in years. We talk daily, but she's busy and not exactly able to pop over for a wine night from her fancy L.A. condo. *Says me, who lives in a fancy SeaTac Condo.*

I send her a quick text as a little update, right after I park in front of Olivia's house.

Molly Wick

Mayday, mayday, may-fucking-day.

Girls' night with all of Levi's friends, and Cal's having boys' night with his dad and the guys.

Pray for me—hope these girls like me and aren't just catty bitches loyal to Levi's history.

The little bubbles pop up before I even close the text thread, and I grin in anticipation. While I wait, I take a moment to admire Olivia's house. It was dark the last time we were here, and while I got a good look at the inside, I didn't get a proper glance at the outside. And holy shit, she did work. The landscaping is immaculate, with flowers blooming in vibrant colors and perfectly trimmed bushes lining the walkway. The house itself is stunning—a single level with high ceilings and large windows.

You got this!

Seriously, don't stress girlie! Everyone who knows you loves you!

But also,

"Here we go," I laugh to myself, grabbing my bag and hefting it over my shoulder.

Before I can knock, the door is being flung open and Ellie is running out toward me.

"Aunnie!" she shouts and barrels into my leg. "Is it okay if I call you that, too? Cal said he calls you that, and I think that's the coolest name ever."

I grin down at her, the little pint-sized girl version of Cal and nod, "I would love that! What's your favorite thing to be called?"

"Princess Ellie-Bennellie Smalls," she says matter-of-factly and I laugh.

"That name is perfect. Who came up with that?"

"Uncle Cooper," she turns and grabs my hand, dragging me the rest of the way to where Olivia is standing in the entryway.

"Sorry, had to send my runner out because, dear lord, am I too pregnant," she says, holding onto her belly. Ellie runs past her, presumably toward her room.

"Oh my gosh, please. If I'd known, I would've just let myself in so you wouldn't have to get up."

She laughs. "It's good for me to be active. My due date is two weeks from now, but I have a feeling this little one will be here sooner than that."

Off to a good start.

I turn the corner, digging in my bag to grab the wine, only to look up and see the kitchen filled with girls—some I met the other night, but others I've only seen in pictures.

"Hi!" I say, holding up the bottle of wine as if it's a sacrificial offering.

"You brought wine!" Odessa says loudly, fist going into the air. "I fucking knew I'd like you."

I let out a huge breath, shoulders relaxing because I am

definitely off to a good start. Also, *holy shit—Odessa Astor is standing in front of me saying she likes me.*

"I actually stole it from Levi's kitchen, so hopefully he doesn't mind," I reply with a grin, feeling a surge of confidence.

"Hopefully he does," Charlie says, walking over and examining the bottle. "There's nothing I love more than ruffling his feathers."

"Hi! I'm Odessa!" She introduces herself as if she isn't one of the most famous people in the entire world, and I can't help but laugh a little.

"Aubrey, so nice to officially meet you! Levi's been sending Cal and me pictures of everyone for so long, I feel like I know all of you."

"Like what?" Olivia asks from her seat at the dining room table.

I nervously glance around the room, realizing the only girl here who hasn't said anything is Maisie, and she's conveniently staying far away from me.

"Uhm," I stammer, "like the rodeo? The day before all the craziness happened, when he was working. There was one of you and Everett, I think you were stuffing cotton candy in his face."

Isla starts laughing so hard, tears welling in her eyes. "He sent me that candid gem too."

"And Charlie, there was one of him holding August while you were glaring at him."

Charlie smirks now. "That little shit put him to sleep in like thirty seconds. I'd been trying for nearly an hour!"

I laugh. "Yeah, he mentioned that."

"Who else? Who else?!" Isla asks eagerly.

I try to think, but I swear Levi could've started a YouTube channel with all the content he sent.

"Lots of Pops, Ellie, and Ben. There was some of the group

at Ponderosa Pine—I think mostly just the guys hitting on women, though."

Odessa laughs. "Sound about right."

"Oh, and lots of desserts from Maisie's," I add, glancing at Maisie. "They looked delicious, by the way."

She nods, offering a somewhat smile but quickly looks away. *Okay, so almost everyone likes me. Also, don't be such a kiss-ass Aubrey.*

Odessa hands me a glass of wine, and I gratefully accept, though I can see the sympathy in her eyes as if she's trying to convey that I shouldn't take offense to Maisie.

"Come sit! Tell us about you," Olivia says, waving her hand toward the table.

I take my seat, mentally bracing myself for the interrogation.

"So uh, well obviously I'm Cal's aunt because Sienna and Levi were together."

Odessa waves her hand in the air. "Yeah, but like, what are you all about? We already know you belong to us—by the way you, one, had the balls to come here, and two, stole a hundred-dollar bottle of wine from Levi."

My jaw drops. "Well, I wasn't aware of the cost, but... that probably wouldn't have stopped me either way."

"Exactly. You already belong."

"Do you work, or has raising Cal been your full-time job?" Odessa asks, and I can tell there's no judgment—only genuine curiosity.

I chuckle. "Raising Cal is definitely a full-time job, but I also have a true-crime podcast called Unsolved Whispers."

Odessa's eyes go wide. "Oh my god, you're A.D.?!"

This time, my eyes widen too. "I—uh, yeah. Aubrey Dubrow."

"Wait, is that the podcast you've been telling us to listen to?" Charlie asks Odessa excitedly.

"Yes! Holy shit! I love your podcast. It's intense but addictive, and I swear I cry every time I listen. There's no YouTube channel though! I would've had no idea you were A.D." Her face is genuinely excited, like I'm the celebrity in the group. "Wait, oh my gosh, say something!" She closes her eyes, listening intently, and I laugh nervously, feeling put on the spot.

"Uh, first, thank you. I really appreciate that. Second, *welcome to Unsolved Whispers, the true crime podcast where secrets fade into silence. I'm A.D, here to uncover the mysteries behind missing persons and all the stories—*" I start, doing my usual podcast intro.

"*That remain unsolved. Stay with me, and listen closely— the truth is out there, waiting to be heard,*" Odessa finishes with more flourish and drama than I usually add.

"I'm absolutely fangirling right now!" she exclaims.

Charlie throws me an impressed look. "So, she's a spooky girl—could've guessed by the tattoos, but I dig it."

I laugh. "Yeah, but I really focus on the storytelling and honoring the victims. Bringing attention to their cases is important to me."

Isla interjects, "Aww, that's so amazing!"

Even Maisie nods slightly, which feels like progress.

"And you live in Seattle, right?" Odessa asks, and I nod. "Tacoma, but yeah, we kind of hate it there."

"The rain?" Charlie asks, prompting Olivia to say, "The gloom?" Then Isla adds, "The doom?" which spurs Odessa into quipping, "Well—clearly, it's not the serial killers."

All of us laugh, and I feel compelled to add, "True, but by the sounds of it, you have your own crazies around here."

"Just another reason to move here—plenty of content!"

"Exactly."

"So," Olivia says, drawing out the word, "I have a secret to get off my chest! Levi told me I was under no circumstances allowed to find you a place to live because he wants you and Cal to live with him."

My jaw drops again, eyes widening in shock. Not that he feels that way—he's made it clear he wants us to move in. It's me on the fence, not wanting to rush it.

"You're joking," Maisie exclaims, looking at Olivia in disbelief.

Olivia shakes her head, a mischievous smile tugging at her lips. "He liiiiii—kes you!"

Charlie laughs. "Oh, he definitely likes her. He already texted me and told me to be nice."

Isla and Odessa both grin from ear to ear. "Me too!" they say in unison.

Again, I notice Maisie is the only one staying quiet, but when she sees us all looking at her, she softly says, "Same."

"Isn't that a little crazy?" I ask them, as if they're my friends and not Levi's.

Isla laughs. "There isn't a single relationship here that didn't start under crazy circumstances. Just another reason you're already one of us."

Her words hit me in a way I wasn't expecting, and tears start to well up.

"I really like him—but Cal. It's so new, you know? Like, what if it doesn't work out, and I mess it all up for Cal?"

All of them shake their heads, but it's actually Maisie who stands up and comes around the table to hug me. "Girl, Levi would never let that happen. He's a good one, and I promise you—he will always be there for you and Cal."

And for whatever reason, the blessing of a few girls I just met feels like enough.

Chapter Twenty-Eight

Levi

"No waaaay! We all have our shit," I hear Odessa saying as I enter the house. "Charlie's is roses, Olivia's gluten-free bread or a miscommunication trope. Isla can't even look at a steak without gagging. Can't put your arm around Maisie without triggering her. And I fucking hate snakes—the reptile and people versions."

"Okay—" I say loudly, announcing myself as I cross into the kitchen. "Time to go home!"

Olivia is the only one that doesn't look like she's been pounding wine all night.

Aubrey giggles when I go straight for her, wrapping my arms around her even though she's sitting.

Loudly enough for everyone to hear, I ask, "How bad were they?"

"Levi Turner!" Olivia admonishes, but I can hear her laugh.

"Not even a little bit. They're seriously the best," Aubrey says.

"Told ya," I say, pulling back enough to wink at her.

"And we all love her!" Odessa chimes in.

"Well, what's not to love?" I reply before grabbing her hand and pulling her up. "Cal's already in the car waiting. He kicked my ass at bowling, I'll have you know."

"Yeah, we go bowling a lot," she says with a shoulder shrug. "Bye—thank you so, so much for including me in girls' night!"

Each of the girls hugs her and me, whispering something about how they like her. By the time we're leaving, I can't stop grinning.

We pass the guys as we head out, and they're coming in, too.

"Thanks for letting them come hang out. Cal's pretty fucking cool—you did good," Hayes tells her, and I can tell that compliment hits higher than most. She takes so much pride in Cal.

I help her out to her car, where Cal is sitting in the backseat playing on his phone. When she gets in, his eyes go slightly wide, before he laughs.

"I love when Aunnie's drunk."

Her mouth drops open, "I am not drunk!"

He laughs, putting his fingers in air quotes, "tipsy."

She looks back at me, then turns around and huffs while she gets buckled. "Maybe a little."

By the time we get back to the house, it's late, and Cal heads right for bed.

I grab Aubrey around the waist before she can go to her own room though, pulling her back into me.

"I missed you," I say into her neck as I hold her.

She giggles again, placing her hands in my hair. "Missed you, too."

"Did you have fun with girls?"

She nods, stepping away, too soon, and I follow right

behind her as she grabs a glass of water. "I really did! I even think I won Maisie over by the end of the night."

"I'd say so, she told me you were great and that she was sorry for being so distant."

Her gaze snaps up to me, looking self-conscious, "she did?"

"She did," I confirm. "The girls loved you."

Her shoulders relax a fraction, as if it was something truly she needed to hear.

"Come to the couch with me?" She glances at the clock, nearing midnight, and I add, "Just for a few minutes. I really did miss you..."

Her lips purse, but she ends up smiling and nodding at my pleading eyes.

When we both settle on the couch, I grab the blanket she's been using the most and drape it over both of us.

"How bad was the interrogation? Did they scare you away forever?"

She laughs. "No, I think they actually helped."

"Helped in what way?" I ask, trying to hide my surprise.

"You know, like with the weirdness of you and me."

"What weirdness?" I ask.

"As in, that you were in love with my sister and now I'm her replacement."

My heart does a strange, uneven stutter at her words—*so self-deprecating*. I can only stare at her for a moment, but then it hits me even harder—especially the realization that the confident girl I know and love might not be as confident as she lets on.

I've suspected it, but I hadn't fully understood the depth— that she would ever feel like Sienna's replacement. When I never even considered it.

The first heartbreak I experienced was losing my mom. Back then, I thought that pain was something I could never recover from. Then Sienna died, and it felt like my world shattered—the thought of losing her and my child was gut-wrenching.

But everything changed when Dan died. Losing my twin, my brother, my best friend—those losses made the others pale in comparison. Suddenly, I realized, they weren't as impossible to endure. Sure, they still hurt, but I'd tucked them into a tiny box in my mind—one smaller than the box I had for Dan.

Now, with Cal in my life, that Sienna box has shrunk even more. My heart is a little more whole.

Being around Aubrey and Cal—my heart doesn't feel so broken anymore.

———

AUBREY

"Did you just say 'her replacement'?" Levi asks, his voice thick with disgust, causing me to cringe slightly.

When I stay silent for a few moments, he reaches for my face, forcing me to meet his gaze. "Aubrey, do you feel like you're Sienna's replacement?" I hear the complete despair in his voice.

"I—" I stammer, searching his face, but he lets go and leans back, eyes on the blank TV screen we never even turned on.

We sit in silence for a moment before he takes a deep breath and shifts on the couch, so he's facing me.

"I don't know how to say this without sounding cold, or harsh, or insensitive—so take from that what you will, but I'm also not going to mince words or my feelings..."

"I would give my life to have Sienna back—for you and Cal —but I wouldn't give your life for hers." His words catch in my throat. "I know Sienna was your sister, and someone I used to date. But the relationship I had with her? It's tiny compared to the one I have with you. I was young, full of myself, oblivious to the real world—and everything that came with it. I won't deny I thought I loved her, but knowing what I know now about life? Everything's different. With you, everything is different."

I absorb his words, tears pooling in my eyes.

"Want to know why? Besides the fact that you're one of the most beautiful women I've ever seen? It's because of how truly selfless you are. I could ask what everyone wants to do for the day, and you'd look around, weighing everyone else's opinions, how it affects them. You care about the underdog, the stories that aren't well known or out there, and you give a voice to all those people. Hell, you're even giving a voice to me."

"I love the way your eyes light up right before a witty comeback, the little tilt of your lips, like you already know it's going to land. I love how you understand Cal, like you two talk without words. And I love that little fidget you do—gripping your bicep, right over your tattoo—sometimes you don't even realize you're doing it. But it's like I can see you gathering the strength to say the hard things, pulling yourself out of that tree —Sienna's tree."

I nod, wiping away the tears. I've never outright said this was for Sienna, but I'm not surprised Levi figured it out.

He gently taps the small bird on the branch in the nest—the one I got to represent Cal.

"I love that you've put them both right here, that the leaves scatter away, but the roots run so deep they disappear. I love that she's as etched into you as she is in me. Because I've fought so long—trying to forget the heartbreak, while trying not to forget them. And now, I feel like I've finally found love again— hope. And it's not because you walked in as a built-in family; it's because of who you are as a person. Because, yeah, I could spend hours with you and Cal, doing family things—and I love that. But I wouldn't mind spending a few more hours after that with you, alone in my bed..." He pauses, winking, and I can't help but laugh as he tries to lighten the mood.

"Aubs, I don't want you to feel second to Sienna, or wonder what my feelings toward her were, or would be if she were still here. I'm not even the same guy I was ten years ago—five years ago. There have been some life-altering, psyche-shifting changes in me and how I see the world. I can't say whether we would've grown together or apart, but I can say I see myself growing with you."

Could I see that, too? Of course I could.

"I could see you and Cal living here, like you've been these last two weeks. I can see us every night, having dinner at that table. I can see us taking Cal to practice, sitting at his games. I can see you going to 'girls' night,' then coming home with a buzz. Do you want that? Any of it?"

"I want it all," I admit, as a warmth spreads through me, feeling the weight of everything lift just a little.

"Good." He smiles, kissing me once before relaxing back into the couch. "And I know it's fast. But trust me—this town roots for the underdog as much as you do. They'll support us. Isla and Everett? Their start was way more intense than ours, and look at them now..."

His mention of Isla and Everett triggers the memory of the girls earlier telling me to go for it. I was already leaning that way, but his words now solidify how I feel and reassure me—once again—that I'm not alone in this.

Cal's been joking about it for days now, already "on to us," despite only sharing a few kisses. But now, it all feels different—real. Like a real commitment.

"Hey, Vi?" I ask softly.

"Yes, Aubs?" He asks, his face quirking as if he's trying to hide the smile threatening to break free.

"Does this mean we get to go try out that bird'ing and bee'ing thing?"

The way his eyes light up, followed by a loud, boisterous laugh, fills my heart.

"Thought you'd never ask."

Chapter Twenty-Nine

Levi

My phone rings at 1 a.m., and I'm already rolling out of bed. It's like my body knew it was time, and I immediately know what's going on—only this time, instead of Dan calling, it's Drew's caller ID.

I don't have time to dwell on how hard that hit. I answer, forcing myself to breathe. "We ready?" I ask him.

He takes a deep, shaky breath, and I hear Olivia say, "Heading in now. Think I still have a little bit of time, though."

"You think?" I demand. "How far apart are—"

"Vi! I don't need you to be my fucking medic right now. I need you to be my brother and get your ass to the hospital waiting room."

"On it. Call me if you need me to deliver a car baby," I say quickly, grabbing my keys and rushing for the door—only to remember Cal and Aubrey are here.

Aubrey and I have spent the last two nights sneaking into my room after Cal goes to bed, only to have her sneak back out and down the hall.

I rush to her door, crack it open, and go in.

Gently, I kiss her forehead. "Hey, baby."

She stirs slightly. "I'm heading to the hospital—Olivia's in labor."

"Oh my god, oh my god, do you need anything?"

"Nah, go back to sleep. I just didn't want you to worry."

I leave, grab my jacket on the way out, and head to my truck. I feel a surge of gratitude for the luxury of a new truck—and how quick it heats up. I hadn't realized I'd care so much, but with the chill in the air, I'm already looking forward to it.

As soon as I pull in, I see Charlie parking in front of me. I back into a spot next to her.

She gets out, dressed in sweats and a sweatshirt, her hair pulled into a bun, and I can't help but laugh as the memory of Olivia in labor with Ellie hits me.

"Thought I was the only one invited to this shindig!"

Charlie laughs loudly, bumping into my shoulder. "Can't believe you were even invited at all!"

I hold up the jacket I brought like a trophy. "Even brought a jacket this time—waiting room sure is cold."

Inside, it's much the same: I walk in and greet most of the staff as if I know them—and a few I actually do.

"Almost seven years later, and guess what? You were a dad this whole time," Charlie says, looking up at me, her eyes welling with emotion. I swear it looks like she's about to cry.

"Who would've thought? It's been—honestly—incredible, though. I'm sad I missed out on so much, but damn, it feels good to have them in my life now."

"You're not going to fuck it up, Vi. You were always meant to be a dad." And then she walks through the door that separates labor and delivery from the waiting room, leaving me nearly in tears myself.

An hour and a half later, Charlie comes out, tears streaming down her face again, and I'm on my feet without hesitation, running to her.

"Again, dammit, they're okay! Everyone's healthy and—yada-yada," she says, sniffling.

"You gotta stop scaring me like that, Charlie-girl!"

"I know, I know. But seeing dads with their new babies? It still gets me—every time. I still cry when Hayes looks at August that way. And Drew's my brother—that used to torture me, and now he's a—" she chokes up again, tears flowing freely, "a dad."

I chuckle, wrapping my arms around her. "It really is magic on earth."

"You ready to meet your new nephew?" she asks, her voice trembling.

"A boy?" I gasp.

She nods, tears falling down her face. "A boy."

She leads me back to their room, and I quickly sanitize my hands before walking in.

Olivia is holding the baby, while Drew stands nearby, gazing at them both.

"I heard we have a boy," I say softly.

"Charles Levi Reynolds," Olivia announces proudly, showing him off, and my jaw drops. "After the best aunt and uncle he could ever have for role models."

Charlie sniffles again beside me, and suddenly I understand the real reason behind all the tears in the waiting room—because this? This is pure, undeniable joy.

———

Aubrey

L evi left in the middle of the night and didn't return until the sun was just starting to rise. I found myself on his front porch, watching the sky lighten, sipping coffee, when I heard his tires crunch down the gravel road.

He gets out—looking all too good in sweats and a sweatshirt. He smiles as he jogs up the steps. "One perfect baby," he says softly.

"And?!" I ask excitedly, eager for the rest.

"Char—" his tone drags out the word, and my eyes go wide —"Les Levi Reynolds, born twenty-two inches and nine and a half pounds."

"Whoa, big baby," I say, genuinely impressed—especially with Olivia. Though, then again, Drew isn't exactly little. "Charles Levi, huh?"

He chuckles, sitting beside me. "Yeah—he's a cutie. You'd think he'd be chunky, but his length really balances him out. And he's got a head full of dark hair—looks like a good mix of mom and dad."

"Aww, I love that for her," I say honestly. It's wild how strong those Turner genes are, but I also think it's pretty sweet that Olivia has her own little one to look like her.

"You ever think about having any of your own?" he asks casually, and I pause, considering.

"I have to be honest, I don't know. I can't say I'd be disappointed either way."

His hand reaches out, taking mine gently. "Cal's enough. Another would be an amazing bonus someday, but I'm also really happy focusing on the relationship I have with him."

I lean my head on his shoulder. "He loves you. He's always been a happy, easy-going kid, but I've never seen him laugh as much as he does when he's around you and everyone. I can see why he feels like he belongs."

"You both belong," he assures me, wrapping his arm around me.

My phone ringing snaps us out of our peaceful moment. Levi looks at me with a raised eyebrow, wondering who could be calling at six in the morning. But I know—Florida's three hours ahead, and I've been expecting this call.

"Do you want some privacy?" he asks softly.

I shake my head. "Would you just stay with me—silent support and all that?"

He nods, and I answer the call. "Hi, Mom."

"Aubrey, are you part of this?" she seethes, and I know she must have been served.

"I—"

"Oh my god, you are! Of course you are! You were so mad that Cal was moving with me to Florida that you involved his sperm donor. And on top of that, I was just served at work! My shift is nearly over, and some woman walks in demanding Rosa Dubrow—do you know how embarrassing that is?!"

I sigh into the phone. "I'm sure that was not a very pleasant experience, but I can't control how the process server does their job."

"Are you kidding me? You started this whole thing! He's fighting me for custody, Aubrey. Did you know that? Of course you do. This was probably all your idea—and his." Her voice drips with venom, and I instantly become defensive.

"Mom, I need you to stop. Really think about your next steps. Levi has every right to press charges against you for fraud, among a laundry list of other things you've done to him. But he won't. Do you want to know why? Because he loves Cal. Not for you. Not for me. For Cal. Because Cal loves you, and he doesn't want to turn Cal against you. But I'm telling you right now—I will. I will explain in detail every lie you've told to his dad, to me, and to him. You have a choice. Accept that Levi is going to be Cal's dad, or face the consequences—you could lose Cal's love and trust forever. It's time to take responsibility for your actions and make amends before it's too late. Because I won't protect you here. What you did to Levi was wrong. And what you did to Sienna? That was wrong too. Whether you thought you were putting Cal first or not, I don't care. It was wrong."

With that, I hang up.

Levi stays silent, his hand resting on my thigh as he stares out at the fields. I feel the weight of my words hanging heavy between us as we sit in silence.

Then he turns to me, eyes sincere. "I really fucking love you."

The honesty in his voice makes my heart swell, lifting me to a new high—where it's just me and him, quietly supporting each other through the hard times.

"I love you, too," I whisper.

Levi's grip on my thigh tightens, his expression softening. "This thing between us? It's not fleeting. It's not only because of Cal," he says quietly, with conviction.

I nod, feeling rooted in his words. Two months ago, I never would have believed that bringing Cal to meet his dad would lead to both of us loving him—and deciding to move here. But here I am, sitting on the porch swing with Levi's arm around me, feeling more loved and at home than I ever have.

Chapter Thirty

Levi

I'm already back at work, dreading my shift and wishing I could be home with Cal and Aubrey. It's been two weeks since we filed the paperwork, and the paternity test has already confirmed—Cal is mine. Obviously, I knew that, but having it on paper felt like final piece.

I begin to walk up the stairs toward the living quarters when the front door swings open behind me, and I turn to see a face I wasn't expecting.

Mr. Calvin—the original Cal—is standing there, eyeing me with a grin on his face.

"Just the man I was looking for," he says, tipping his head up.

I fully turn, stepping back down the stairs as he continues, "You got a second to talk?"

I nod, fighting the grin threatening to spread across my face.

"You know, son," he says, raising an eyebrow, "I heard a rumor around town the other day."

Playing dumb, I say, "Small towns and those rumors—can't believe most of 'em."

He smirks. "So you're saying you don't have a teenage son that looks just like you and is named Cal?"

My shoulders lift in a shrug, but I can't hide the grin anymore. "Not a teen yet."

He chuckles. "Well, I'll be damned—looks like you've finally fulfilled an age-old debt, huh?"

I smirk back. "Did you ever really doubt I would?"

"No. I just figured you'd get out of it by never having kids. I'm happy for you—and the redhead?"

I let out a deep sigh. "That's a little more complicated. She's Cal's biological aunt—who raised him. His mom died from complications of an embolism when she was pregnant with him."

"Wow—I'm sorry. And you had no idea?"

"None," I admit, then launch into the story. If there's anyone I trust with this, it's Mr. C—he's always been a good friend and mentor.

He shakes his head in disbelief. "I can't imagine finding out something like that."

"Feel free to set the record straight," I say, "so the rumor mill doesn't go wild."

Guess that's one problem down.

An hour later, the call comes in—dispatcher's voice sharp and urgent.

"Six-year-old girl, fallen from a tree. Victim's in need of medical assistance—scene's chaotic. We have units en route. Be advised, victim's father is belligerent and refusing help. Trooper on scene has been advised to stage nearby."

Jed and I exchange a quick glance, then start to gear up.

He's been working more now that his baby is a bit older, but he's still relatively new to being licensed, and I typically run the calls we go on.

"Goin' disco?" He asks, meaning lights and sirens.

I nod, "for now."

We pull out, the sirens wailing as we head in the direction of the address I recognize from memory. It's a few miles outside of town; the house and driveway run parallel to the highway if I'm correct.

Jed focuses on the road, steady hands on the wheel, while I try to reach dispatch for updates.

"Girl was climbing a tree, fell out—possible broken arm," Paige responds. "Witness saw it, called it in. Marzollo was closest. Units about five minutes out. Still advising to stage."

I nod, eyes still on the road. We pull up a few yards from the driveway, waiting for the all-clear. On the other side of the road, the woman who called it in stands near her car—classic Karensque—blonde, perfectly curled hair, designer sunglasses, phone pressed to her ear with an annoyed expression.

"Fuck," Jed mutters next to me, and I turn my gaze toward the scene.

Fuck, is right. Immediately, I recognize the 'dad'—Sonny King, known around here for leading a local biker gang. He's clutching his daughter, Sammy, tight in his arms, glaring at the trooper who's trying to keep a safe distance but looks ready for trouble. Behind Sonny, three other men in cuts with patches stand tense, hands dangerously close to their waistbands, fingers brushing near their guns.

"I know them," I mutter to Jed as I reach for the door handle, ready to step out and try to diffuse this. The daughter, Sammy, went through pre-school with Ellie and was in her Kindergarten class.

His arm shoots out, stopping me. "We're staging, Vi."

I glance back at the chaos. They don't have minutes for deputies to arrive. Sonny's face is red, twisted with rage, yelling at the solo trooper—raw, threatening. And the worst part, Trooper Marzollo isn't backing down. If anything, it looks like he's making things worse.

"I'm going," I say firmly. "Tell dispatch to tell Luke it's Sammy."

I don't know Sonny well, but from volunteering at Ellie's school, I've seen Trisha—his wife—a kind, caring nurse who works at the town's nursing home. I've heard snippets about Sonny, and none of them are good.

Slowly, deliberately, I walk toward the scene, hands raised in peace.

"FUCK YOU, PIG!" Sonny screams as he yells at Marzollo, the Oregon State Trooper who's had that big ego and mean scowl for years. Normally, I get along with him just fine, but today I want to hit him simply for not knowing how to deescalate this.

"King," I shout, keeping my tone casual, "How's it going over here?"

All eyes turn to me, hands gripping guns—*not so concealed anymore.* Sammy looks terrified in her dad's arms, eyes wide, panicked, darting around.

"The fuck you want Turner?"

It takes all of me not to get worked up, to let him affect me the way he wants. Instead I say, "Heard your daughter took a little fall—only want to check to make sure she's alright and then I'll be on my way."

"Fuck you, Turner!" *This fucking guy.*

"I know, man. I get it—you didn't call askin' for help. But, someone did, and State-y isn't just gonna let this go."

Their attention swings back to Marzollo, who somehow

244

manages to look even more like a dick—standing taller, chest puffed out.

Sensing the shift in energy, I soften my tone. "Hey, Sammy, right?"

She looks at her dad, then at me—hesitant. "Hi, Mr. Levi."

Her dad's head rears back, a new facial expression crossing his features—a mix of "I'll fucking kill you" and "What the fuck?"

"How the hell do you—"

I cut him off quickly. "My niece is Ellie. She's friends with Sammy. Trish and her came to Ellie's birthday party last year, right?" I ask, glancing at Sammy, keeping my tone relaxed and confident.

Sammy nods. "And Mr. Levi helped me at the end-o-school-year party."

I fake a grin. "Oh, yeah. You crashed hard in that tricycle race, huh?"

Sammy gives a small smile, eyes still full of fear.

Sonny's grip on her loosens just slightly, accepting the recognition to be innocent.

Suddenly, the trooper—who's clearly not the sharpest tool —yells, "King, you let him assess her, or I'll arrest you for impeding an investigation."

I spin on him, something I shouldn't do considering my back is now to men who probably still want to shoot me.

"Why don't you go talk to whoever called it in? Luke's on his way. He'll handle King," I say sharply, shooting Marzollo an annoyed glare. He glares right back, but after a moment, he nods once and walks back toward the road, approaching the driver still standing outside her BMW.

King scoffs behind me. "Fuck you, Turner—and fuck Haynes. Trish'll be here in a minute."

I turn back, suddenly feeling drained at this guy constantly cussing me out. "Look, King, I'm going to shoot straight with you. You either let me evaluate Sammy—make sure she doesn't have internal bleeding, a concussion, or a hundred other silently deadly injuries—or I walk away and involve CPS. And if you think Trish won't kick both of our asses for that, then you're about as smart as Trooper Marzollo."

That gets a small chuckle from the shorter guy behind him. King hesitates for a second, then nods.

I motion behind me for Jed to move forward, and he does, the sirens already in the distance. I pray whoever's coming doesn't screw this up worse.

"Hey, Sammy," I say softly. "Want to see the back of an ambulance? It's pretty cool—lots of shiny things and buttons they say I'm not supposed to touch, but sometimes I do. Or Dad can set you on the back of his truck, and I can grab my bag."

Jed parks next to King's jacked-up Dodge Ram and steps out cautiously.

Sammy's eyes widen at the sight of the ambulance, and she almost smiles. "Can I see the back of the ambulance?"

King sighs but nods, gently setting her down. She gingerly holds her arm away from her side and walks toward me. I lead her to the back of the ambulance.

"This is Jed," I say, gesturing toward him. "He's kind of my helper."

Jed rolls his eyes next to me, standing at the back doors.

I start to show Sammy some of the gear inside while asking her little questions about what happened. Her dad stands across from us, glaring, arms crossed.

"So, you like to climb?"

She nods, looking sheepishly at her dad. "Mom doesn't let me, but Dad will if he's outside."

I check her arm while she talks—doesn't look broken. Scraped, definitely, but only superficial cuts.

"I used to love climbing—rock wall climbing, that is—when I was your age," I say, as I begin gently palpating her arm, feeling for any tenderness or abnormal movement.

"Mom would never let me!"

I chuckle. "There's a place in Bend with indoor climbing. They'll fit you with a harness and rope to keep you safe. Maybe next time, you can ask your dad to take you."

She nods happily as I finish my assessment. "Sounds cool."

Suddenly, I hear another commotion behind us: "Fuck you, Haynes. This is private property!"

I catch the telltale sign of a long sigh. "King—are those just your standard greetings now?"

"Don't trust your kind."

"Same." Luke says exasperated. "I'm only here to make sure Sammy's okay and to cuss out my paramedic who can't follow simple fucking rules."

I turn around, grinning. "You always say that 'all we do is stage.' Now you're mad we didn't stage?"

"Turner, I swear to God, I will have you fired."

King chuckles beside him, and everyone seems to relax at the banter.

I turn back around and help Sammy out of the ambulance.

"Obviously, I'm not a doctor, but nothing looks broken," I tell King. "Trish will want to debride it and get any dirt out, but it's just some minor cuts."

He looks at me, and for the first time, I see him as a worried dad.

Suddenly, Trish King rounds the open door of the ambulance, her voice high-pitched and furious. "God dammit, King! What the hell? You let her climb that tree?!"

King shrinks back a fraction as she storms over, scooping up her daughter and cooing softly.

He tries to defend himself. "I was right there, babe! She's fine—she's good at it—ya know? You should see how fast—"

He stops when Trish's eyes nearly bug out of her head.

"Sorry," he mutters, and Trish turns to Sammy, wrapping her in a warm hug and softly cooing to her.

She looks at me. "How bad?"

"I was just telling King—she's fine. Clean the wound up really good, and I think she'll be okay. You know the things to watch out for?"

She nods, then I turn to Luke, who looks pissed as hell.

"Come on, boss. You can chew me out back at the station." He's not actually my boss, but I have a feeling I'll be getting a lecture from both.

Chapter Thirty-One

Levi

My phone rings just as I'm about to get into my truck, and I smile when I see it's Aubrey. It's been a long forty-six-hour shift—from dealing with the Kings to two visits to Loretta's—and I'm looking forward to heading home and relaxing with my family.

"Hey, Aubs. I'm heading home now," I answer.

She huffs out a loud breath. "Well, don't. My mom's in town."

"At our house?!"

"No, she's meeting us here at Ponderosa for dinner."

I blink, trying to process that. "Meeting us... for dinner at Ponderosa?" I repeat slowly, as if I didn't hear her right. Because why on earth would she say something so normal when everything else feels so absolutely messed up?

"If you're okay with it—Cal and I can go alone. I thought you might want to be part of the conversation. She seemed—I don't know—apologetic? I could be wrong, but I thought she might want to make amends."

I hesitate, then quickly reply, "I'll meet you there," before I can second-guess myself. I don't trust Rosa for a second alone with them, especially knowing how manipulative she can be.

Thankfully, the station is close, and I'm pulling into the parking lot when I see Cal and Aubrey leaning against her car —no Rosa in sight.

I hop out, jogging over and pulling Aubrey into a quick hug. "You good?"

She nods against me, and I glance at Cal. "Ready for an epic parental battle over who gets you for Christmas?"

He laughs and rolls his eyes. "Aunnie wins. Always."

I chuckle. "Thank God she's on my team, then."

A black SUV pulls in just as we're talking, and we all look up, as if we somehow knew it was her.

She steps out—a sleek black dress hanging on her like she's going to a funeral. But I have to admit, she hasn't aged a day since I last saw her—like they injected her with embalming fluid to keep her forever young. *Probably made a deal with the devil.*

Cal's smile is genuine when he sees her. He walks over and hugs her, whispering something that makes her crack a smile.

She looks right at me, then at Aubrey, then back again, her expression unreadable.

"I'm not going to kiss your feet, if that's what you're expecting," she mumbles with a smirk.

"Mom!" Aubrey scolds, but I only laugh, pulling Aubrey close again. She's going to be my lifeline, keeping me grounded.

"Come on, Ms. Dubrow. We've got a lot of catching up to do," I say, voice light with the playful tone I can't help slipping into.

We all walk into Ethan's restaurant, and every face turns to stare—of course, recognizing me immediately. Callie, the manager, is waiting at the front, her eyes widening when she sees us, bouncing between all of us with obvious surprise. I bet she's already heard the story—even though I told Mr. C to fill everyone in just days ago.

As we approach the hostess stand, I feel the weight of everyone's eyes on us. Callie's greeting is polite but cautious, her head nodding in acknowledgment as she quickly leads us to a quiet booth in the back.

I gesture for Aubrey to go in first, then take the seat next to her. Cal does the same for Rosa, sitting across from me. That's good—seeing him across from me keeps me sane, keeps me calm.

Cal breaks the silence first. "So, what brings you to town, Grandma?"

Aubrey's hand quickly covers her mouth as she hides a laugh, and I feel myself chuckling too.

"Of course I'm here to visit my favorite grandson," she replies with a twinkle in her eye.

Cal grins, pleased.

"And," she continues, "to do some good old-fashioned apologizing and groveling."

I do my best to hide my shock—exactly not what I expected to hear.

"What brought you to your senses?" I ask, voice steady but firm.

She twitches her lips, exchanging a look with me before she admits, "Besides Aubrey's little scolding... I got a call from someone you may know."

"Who's that?"

"Think my grandson here calls him 'Pops.'"

My stomach tightens, and I have to school my expression so it doesn't betray my surprise. Aubrey doesn't get the memo, and gasps loudly next to me.

"Zeke called you?" she demands, disbelief edging her voice.

"Called me, gave me an earful," she dismisses, waving her hand.

Cal grins again. "I knew it'd work."

"You were in on it?" Aubrey turns sharply to him.

He shrugs, acting casual despite the obvious tension. "I just suggested he call—grandparent to grandparent."

"And it worked?" Her eyes narrow, doubt flickering in her tone.

Her mom waves dismissively. "Well, I'm not a totally inhumane, soulless human being. I may have made mistakes in the past, but I'm not incapable of seeing them, of trying to make things right." Her words linger in the air, tinged with defensiveness beneath the veneer.

"I never said that," Aubrey quickly cuts in, watching her. "But you were so stubborn about Cal moving to Florida."

Rosa exhales sharply, muttering, "I didn't want Cal to know what I did. Someone was blackmailing me—"

"Blackmailing?!" Aubrey's voice jumps, her eyes widening in shock.

Her mom waves her hand again, dismissive. "Emails regarding a law firm I worked with. It was nothing, really. I was worried they'd contact Cal, tell him what I did, and... you."

I remain silent, watching Aubrey's gaze bounce between her mother and Cal. There's a flicker of hurt, betrayal—something raw in her eyes.

"You know everything now?" she asks softly.

Cal nods slowly, guilt writ plain on his face. "Grandma called me yesterday when I was with Pops. He encouraged me to answer, so I did. That's why I wasn't surprised she was coming to town."

Aubrey turns away, gazing out the window in silence. I see the conflict flickering across her face—hurt mingled with confusion, betrayal.

"I'm sorry, Aunnie," Cal finally says softly. "I knew if we all got in the same room, we could figure this out. Okay?"

She turns back, her expression torn—caught between anger and understanding.

"And look," Cal adds, "we're here, and Grandma said I don't have to move to Florida anymore."

Both Aubrey and I turn to Rosa, who wears that overly innocent "see, I'm a good person" expression that part of me still wants to hate.

But I stay quiet, trying to process everything. Can I ever really like Rosa Dubrow? Probably not. But maybe I can be cordial—for Cal's sake.

She clears her throat, her voice trembling just a little. "So, I guess this is the apology part. I'm sorry for the way I treated you when Sienna was—" She pauses, her face suddenly clouded with grief.

I see her—really see her—again, twelve years ago in the hospital, devastated. Maybe this is the first time I recognize her as the grieving mother who lost her daughter, and it hits a little harder now that I have Cal and understand the physical pain of losing someone so close. I lost Sienna at the time, but I'd only known her for a few months. Losing Dan—that pain for me— was the equivalent of her losing her child. Her weakest moment, the tragedy that changed the course of her life.

I think back to the things I did and said when Dan died— moments I'm not proud of—and am thankful for the grace my family gave me. *Can I do that?*

"I *am* sorry—for not being more transparent about her diagnoses—and about Cal too. I know you'll never forgive me, and I don't expect you to."

All I can do is nod—acknowledging her words, even if they're just words. It's a fairly good apology, all things considered.

When I glance over, Cal looks nervously between us, the tension clear in his posture. Is holding a grudge worth hurting Cal? No—not even a little bit.

"You know, Ms. Dubrow," I say softly, "it rained in my head for years with all of the heartache. But now, if only you could see behind it all—wildflowers."

Epilogue

Aubrey

Three months later—

"Levi, where are you taking me?" he offered to take me and Cal to dinner tonight, but Cal decided he'd rather have more fun with Pops. Now we're driving through Bend, and I'm still trying to remember the roads, to find the landmarks I once knew. It's been so long since I lived here, and after our initial trip, I realized how much the city had changed—new developments, shops I didn't recognize, neighborhoods that had blossomed from empty lots. Bend's landscape still feels familiar, like an old friend, but the city has grown into something sprawling and vibrant, with mountain views that never get old. *Although, the views are even more grand in Three Sisters.*

"I may have done a surprise thing," Levi says casually, "that you're either going to love or hate."

My jaw drops. *Surely he doesn't mean proposing?* Knowing Levi, it very well could be. He moved us right into it—things have been wonderful and amazing—but marriage? Come on.

The next question—*would I say no?* Nope—and what does

that say about me? I'm crazy, madly, deeply in love with Levi Turner. He's funny and outgoing, loving and kind, serious and sensitive—*and great in bed.*

Our life has felt full—like Cal and I had been drifting through the years, just the two of us—and occasionally, my mom—not knowing how it could be any other way. Then, all of a sudden, we have this huge, crazy, beautiful family. They do TNT-D dinners with the core Turner family, along with Sunday night dinners with the entire clan. It's—I don't even have words to describe how special that is, how unique, how blessed I feel to be welcomed into this incredible family.

Levi turns down a somewhat familiar road, and I stare in awe as we weave through a neighborhood I definitely remember—quaint streets lined with tall evergreens and houses with stucco siding, some freshly painted, others beginning to show signs of age. It's the kind of neighborhood that feels secluded, yet your neighbor is right next to you.

Then he parks his truck in front of a house I definitely remember—the house my mom bought, the one Sienna, my mom, and I lived in together. She may have moved out the year she died, but she still had a room there.

I often wondered what happened to her things—why did it always feel like only half our house had been shipped to us? The house stands quietly, freshly painted but the same color, its windows reflecting the late afternoon sun. It's been years, but it looks exactly the same, as if time has stood still here—or perhaps just moved too fast for me to keep up.

"Why are we here?" I ask, nearly feeling out of the breath with the overwhelming feelings of seeing this house.

"I called your dad." Levi admits softly, and I whip around to look at him, shocked he did that and how it has anything to do with this house.

"You did?"

"I did," Levi nods. "And I know it's been a few months, and we've mostly forgiven your mom—but there's things you need to know."

I nod, feeling confused but maybe a little relieved. "Okay? I need—the short version. Blurt it all out, no codes. What is going on?"

Levi nods, smiling at my directness. "I called your dad about two weeks ago. It took him less than an hour to call back, and when he did, he explained everything. He bought this house from your mom, apparently kept everything the same," he says, nodding toward the house, seeing what I see. It all looks the same—down to the three white rocking chairs on the front porch.

He continues, "on one condition—he wasn't allowed to reach out to you. You could call him, contact him, but he wasn't allowed to call you. He agreed because he wanted to keep the memories you had here—he was upset with how your mom was cutting him out of the decisions with Sienna. He wasn't allowed at the hospital either. He tried to pull the same favors I did, but your mom was—well, your mom."

I nod, tears spilling down my cheeks. "Why didn't he answer when I called?"

"Your mom blocked his number from your account. It wasn't him blocking you; it was, technically, you blocking him. It never went through because he was blocked by the account holder."

"God—my fucking mother!" I lean back, my head hitting the headrest harshly.

Levi gently grabs the back of my head, massaging it. "We already expected this, right? Yes, it's now the truth in the open. But I know you were too afraid to ask her, and I'm not exactly texting pals with her either."

I nod, looking back at him. His blue eyes plead with me.

"You have a right to be mad, to tell her off, to feel how you want to feel. But today, today I need you to put that aside."

"Why?"

"Because your dad misses you, and I think you should focus on repairing today," Levi says, gesturing toward the house again. When I look, I see my dad standing on the porch of the house he never lived in—but paid for... *twice.* He's dressed in his signature slacks and a button-down shirt.

"I'll be with you the whole time."

I get out of the car, and instantly nerves hit me. *Is this how Cal felt?* It's different, but all those doubts flood into my mind. *Will it be awkward? Does he hate me? Does he want me in his life?*

"Hi, Aubbie," he says softly, his voice gentle but steady, before walking to meet me halfway and pulling me into a hug.

He looks older—more gray in his hair, lines deeper around his eyes—but somehow, he still smells the same, a familiar blend of citrus and sandalwood that instantly surfaces memories I thought I'd buried.

"Hi, Dad."

I pull away slightly, rubbing at my nose, which feels unexpectedly tingling. Emotions threaten to spill over, but I hold them back, trying to stay steady.

My dad reaches out and extends a hand to Levi, who takes it without hesitation. "David Dubrow," my dad says sincerely, his voice thick with emotion. "You'll never know how much it means to me that you brought my daughter to me."

Levi, ever the quick wit, offers a smirk. "Actually, sir," he replies evenly, "I believe I know exactly how you feel."

Epilogue-2

Aubrey

Four years later—

OH. MY. GOD.
"Cal Sullivan Dubrow!"

Cal hops out of the driver's side of Levi's old truck, holding a small, rectangular piece of paper high in the air like it's a trophy. The paper fluttered slightly in the late afternoon breeze, catching the light in a way that makes it look like a treasure. That truck—Levi and Cal had spent nearly three years working on it together—tuning every part, fixing what was broken, and making it their own. And just last month, Levi and I had gifted it a fresh paint job for Cal's sixteenth birthday, the same royal blue and white that made it stand out on the road back in it's prime.

"Liii—censed!" Cal's voice rings out, loud and proud. His grin stretches from ear to ear, the proud almost-adult that he's becoming shining through his eyes.

Levi rounds the other side of the truck, a matching grin spreading across his face as he watches Cal with pride. Tears cloud my vision, threatening to spill over—part happiness, part nostalgia, all love.

"You did it!" Cal hugs me fiercely, towering over me, yet still somehow conveying an innocence that makes my heart ache.

"Of course, Aunnie," Cal responds confidently, still holding the paper high. "Did you doubt me? Me?"

I chuckle at his unwavering pride, and Levi laughs along with me. "Yeah, Aunnie!" Levi teases, mimicking Cal's tone with a grin.

These two have been peas in a pod since day one, and I wouldn't want it any other way. It's almost laughable that I spent so long thinking Levi was a deadbeat dad, when in reality, he's the best. He loves Cal fiercely—and me, as well.

"You meeting us there?" Levi asks him, and I feel a pit settle in my stomach. I was so excited for Cal to get his license; I hadn't fully thought about him being out on his own, driving by himself.

A grin spreads across Cal's face when he sees me. "Yep. Promise I'll drive safe!" Then he turns around and walks off, acting like it's no big deal. There's an entire party waiting for him at Olivia's house—friends, family, balloons, the works—all to celebrate his sixteenth birthday.

"We just let him go?" I ask, surprised.

"The state of Oregon says he's ready," Levi replies confidently. "He's been driving with me every day for the last year. He's got this, babe."

Sighing, I follow behind, but then I notice Levi walking a little faster toward his own truck.

"You in a hurry?" I call out.

He turns around with a grin. "Yeah, move your butt, Turner! We can't follow him if he's miles ahead of us!"

Cal's birthday dinner is winding down, but everyone's still here, celebrating him. The house is alive with "aunts," "uncles," and "cousins," all laughing and mingling. Olivia and Drew have Ben, who's now twelve—and still thinks Cal is the coolest person ever—Ellie, who just turned ten, and Charles, who celebrated his fourth birthday last month. Charlie and Hayes's little ones include August, and Coraline—an adorable yet feisty two-year-old. Isla and Everett welcomed Luna just six months ago, while Odessa and Luke are proud parents of twin boys, Roscoe and Ruben. Maisie and Ethan have Jake, who's ten, and Maisie is due next month with a girl.

It's chaos, in the best way.

I find myself in the kitchen, pouring a drink, finally able to breathe a little easier after making sure Cal's celebration was in full swing. It's a moment of reflection for me—thinking about the last four years. Everyone here looks happy, content, fulfilled —and married. I feel so lucky, knowing I was at every single one of their weddings—except Charlie and Hayes's—and that they were there for Levi and me.

Levi once called this a "made family," and I hadn't truly understood what that meant—until I became part of it. It's loud and opinionated, fiercely protective and unwaveringly loyal. It's a tangled web of love and madness, where every smile and scuffle only makes us stronger, bonded not by blood, but by choice.

Just as I lift my glass to take a sip, Odessa gasps loudly and demands, "You can't drink that!"

"What?!" I gasp instinctively, my surprise evident.

"You—You can't—do you?" Her face drains of all color, and she looks around, realizing the kitchen is crowded. She quickly grabs my arm, pulling me as she hustles out of the room.

She drags me into the bathroom, shuts the door behind us, and turns the water on.

"What are you doing?" I ask, confused.

"You're pregnant," she says matter-of-factly. Of course, I know that, but there's no way she does. No one does. I'm barely six weeks along, and I haven't even told my husband.

"What makes you think that?" I ask, my voice tense.

"You're—uh—I mean, I don't want to say anything too soon."

"Odessa Astor, what the hell does that mean?!" I demand, my voice sharp.

She sighs and pleads, "It's—okay, please don't judge me."

I nod silently, waiting for her to explain.

"So, you know how there's been a lot of pregnancies and babies lately?"

"Uh, yeah?"

"Well, I've been noticing something... weird."

"What are you talking about?"

"It's like this gut feeling? And, uh, you're—well, you're silver."

"I'm what?!" I explode.

She groans, frustrated. "I don't know! You're like silver—maybe a little orange. When I saw you, I felt it. Not like saw it with my eyes—I don't know how to explain—but it's like that same feeling I had six months ago with Isla, and with the twins, Maisie right now, Charlie. Pregnant women—I feel the color silver."

"You feel it?" I repeat, incredulous.

"It's so freaking weird, right?"

"Uh, yeah, Dess, it's weird as hell. But you're not wrong."

She gasps, eyes wide. "You're pregnant?!"

I nod, and tears fill Odessa's eyes before they go wide. "Then why the hell are you drinking?!"

"It's non-alcoholic! I dumped out the original and poured it into that bottle at home. Then I got rid of the evidence because Levi doesn't know yet!"

"What's going on in there?" Olivia asks from the other side.

Odessa's eyes go even wider, and she quickly turns, opening the door. She yanks Olivia inside and closes it behind her.

Olivia looks at the water, then at me. "What happened?"

With a heavy sigh, I mumble, "I'm pregnant."

"You're what?!" Olivia demands, eyes wide.

Another voice calls from outside the door, and Odessa, once again alert, opens it to see Charlie and Isla.

"We saw her go in! We want to come in, too!" they both say in unison.

I laugh, taking a step back.

"No loud gasps, no yelling—zip those lips!" I tease.

They all nod eagerly. "Levi doesn't know, I'm freaking the hell out because he's going to lose it."

"About what?" Charlie asks, concern clear in her voice.

"I'm six weeks pregnant."

Both Charlie and Isla's eyes go even wider, then they break into big smiles.

"PREGNANT?!"

"Yes," I confirm. "And Levi's going to lose his mind with worry. I can barely catch a cold without him fussing over me."

"Aww," Olivia makes a face, but Odessa bursts into laughter.

"It's not the same, Aubs," Charlie reassures me gently. "I mean, you're pregnant, but it won't be the same as it was for Sienna. We'll make sure he knows that, okay?"

Odessa nods, her eyes gleaming. "Say the word, and we'll whisk you away for some girl time—away from his hovering."

Suddenly, a loud knock from outside the door. "Uhm, hello? Why wasn't I invited to this 'Spilling Tea' session?!"

Of course, it's Levi. At the sound of his voice, every single one of us gasps simultaneously, exchanging looks, realizing we've been caught.

"I'll lie!" Odessa whispers quickly. "Say I needed to ask about BV or something."

I can't help but giggle. "Odessa, you don't need to lie about having bacterial vaginosis for me, but I really appreciate you being willing to do it." I take a deep breath, feeling strength grow from each woman around me.

"Hello?!" Levi calls again, knocking a little softer.

"You're all the very best friends I could ask for, and I know Levi feels the same about each of you," I say softly. "On the count of three, Charlie, open the door, and we all say it together?"

The energy shifts as Odessa, Charlie, and the others smile, excitement lighting up their faces.

"One." Charlie's hand reaches for the handle.

"Two." I can't believe how anxious I am—he's going to freak out that we're yelling this at him.

"Three." Charlie opens the door, revealing Levi and all the other husbands, standing there staring at us.

"I'm pregnant!" I yell at the exact same moment the girls shout, "She's pregnant!"

The shocked expressions on all their faces quickly melted into a cacophony of cheers. If Levi was freaking out, he didn't show it. If anything, he looked—excited, happy, overjoyed—completely in love.

This—this is the dream. The beautiful life, the treasured memories that shape us—the strength of family support.

Family isn't always blood; it's built from choice, vulnerability, and love that refuses to waver.

And if there's one piece of advice I'd give freely—it's to find those people. The ones who will search for you when you run away. The ones who will love you—the good, the bad, and the hurt. The ones who fight every day to remind you that you are loved and important. The ones willing to wait a lifetime for a chance with you. Most importantly, find the people who cheer so loudly for you that you don't even notice the ones who aren't.

Acknowledgments

First and foremost, I want to thank my husband, Matt. From the moment I said, "I think I want to write a book," he supported me wholeheartedly. There wasn't a doubt in his mind that I could accomplish it—and now, look: a full-blown series! He's helped me through every writer's block, been my sounding board, but most importantly, he's cheered the loudest. Without him, I wouldn't have had the courage to pursue this career or discover my true calling.

To my sister, Katie—you were the first-ever reader, and for that, you gave me the confidence to keep going. Your notes of "10/10" and "HAWT" were exactly the encouragement I needed to embark on this journey, resulting in my debut series —all six books of it!

To my mom, Julie—thank you for spending hundreds (maybe thousands) of dollars at Barnes & Noble throughout my childhood. You fostered a love of reading that led me to living out a dream.

To the rest of my family—your unwavering love, patience, and support mean everything to me. My sweet grandmothers, who cheer me on and are willing to read my books despite the colorful language and innuendos. Every cousin and aunt who reads, promotes, and recommends—you are part of the reason I have so many wonderful readers!

A special thank you to my editor, Sam Moon, for your invaluable feedback and for helping shape this series into something I'm truly proud of. You're the best, and I can't recommend you enough to all those aspiring authors out there!

To my friends who never complain when I ask off-the-wall questions—thank you for listening, for your helpful advice, and for always cheering me on. I feel so blessed to have friends willing to answer every question, from police work (Zack Johnson), to snowboarding down mountains (Chasen Schultz.), to logging terminology (Kaitlyn Kronberger).

To my readers—thank you for your belief in these stories and for allowing me to share their journeys with you. Your encouragement and enthusiasm inspire me every single day! With an even bigger shout out to Brittny Rubin @thebookedlifewithbritt, Addison Thames, Shelby Kronberger, Ash @all_ashs_chapters—you've all sent messages during times of self-doubt that encouraged me to keep going.

And finally, to my characters—thank you for inspiring me with your stories, struggles, and love. You feel like family, and I'm grateful to have had the opportunity to tell your stories.

Here's to many more stories and adventures ahead.

Speaking of which, stay tuned for details on my next series: *The High Desert's Edge.*

Also by TJ Deal

About the Author

TJ Deal is a Pacific Northwest-based aspiring author who often daydreams about writing stories in the incredible places she travels to around the world. Thanks to her husband's unwavering support and her lifelong obsession with reading, she has decided to follow her passion for writing. Her days are mostly spent drinking coffee, relishing in the daily grind of motherhood, and capitalizing on every free moment to work on her latest novel.

www.ingramcontent.com/pod-product-compliance
Lightning Source LLC
Chambersburg PA
CBHW032237310726

48973CB00008B/2185